WOMEN

WOMEN
A NOVEL ABOUT POLISH LIFE

ZOFIA NAŁKOWSKA

Volume 1 of the Young Poland Revisited Series

Translation Revised and Edited by Jack J. B. Hutchens

MODERN BARBARIAN
PRESS

Women: A Novel about Polish Life
by Zofia Nałkowska ©2024
This text is based on the 1906 Polish original in consultation with the 1920 translation by Michael Henry Dziewicki, both now in the public domain.
Published by Modern Barbarian Press
Champaign, Illinois and Poznań, Poland

Cover art from Art Goût Beauté
Cover design by Jack J. B. Hutchens

ISBN 13: 978-0-9791236-7-2

Contents

Introduction
Nałkowska, the Young Poland Movement, and *Women*

The turn of the twentieth century witnessed the emergence of a vibrant cultural and artistic movement in Poland known as Young Poland (Młoda Polska). Occurring at a time when Poland as a free nation had not existed for 100 years, it was characterized by a fervent desire for artistic renewal and societal transformation, giving rise to a multitude of talents across various disciplines. Among the prominent figures of this period was Zofia Nałkowska (1884-1954), a trailblazing Polish writer whose literary contributions played a crucial role in shaping the intellectual landscape of her time.

Young Poland, spanning roughly from the 1890s to the outbreak of World War I, marked a departure from the previous generations' conservatism as embodied in the Positivist movement. Embracing modernism and the avant-garde, Young Poland sought to break free from the shackles of tradition and explore new horizons in literature, art, and philosophy. This movement was not confined solely to Poland; it resonated with similar cultural shifts occurring across Europe.

The Young Poland movement encompassed a diverse array of artistic expressions, including literature, visual arts, music, and theater. Artists and intellectuals associated with this movement sought to inject vitality into Polish culture by embracing international trends while preserving the nation's unique identity.

Nałkowska emerged as a key figure within the literary scene of Young Poland. Born in 1884 in Warsaw, Nałkowska exhibited a prodigious literary talent from an early age. Her writing, characterized by its depth, social consciousness, and psychological insight, reflected the tumultuous times in which she lived.

Nałkowska's early works, such *Kobiety* (Women, 1906), demonstrated her experimentation with various literary styles and themes. However, it was her later works that solidified her reputation as a formidable writer. *Border* (Granica, 1910), a novel exploring the complexities of human relationships, garnered critical acclaim for its innovative narrative structure and psychological depth.

One of Nałkowska's most significant contributions to literature was her slim collection of eight short stories based on interviews with victims and perpetrators of the Holocaust. In 1945, she was elected President of the Commission for the Investigation of War Crimes at Auschwitz. From this experience she would produce *Medallions* (Medaliony, 1946, translated and published by Northwestern University Press in 2000), which has become one of the most important pieces of Holocaust literature.

Kobiety

One of Nałkowska's earliest works is the trilogy *Women,* a profound exploration of female experience at a crucial juncture in history when she was just twenty-two. Published early in the century against the backdrop of societal upheavals and the growing feminist movement, the novel stands as a poignant and complex portrayal of women's lives, aspirations, and struggles.

The characters of *Women* are not mere archetypes; they are complex individuals whose stories resonate with authenticity. Nałkowska's narrative skillfully navigates the intricacies of female relationships, highlighting the bonds of solidarity and the tensions arising from societal expectations. Through their experiences, the novel unfolds as a compelling exploration of the intersections of gender, class, and identity.

Women is a powerful work of social critique, illuminating the patriarchal structures that circumscribe women's lives. It engages with the feminist discourse of the time, challenging traditional roles and advocating for women's autonomy and agency. Urszula Chowaniec sees Nałkowska as offering in her novel "a new model of a woman liberated from the constraints of the male world," arguing that "women should get rid of the male glorification of femininity."[1] The theme of resilience and the pursuit of self-realization permeates the narrative. Nałkowska does not shy away from portraying the harsh realities faced by her characters, but within their struggles, she finds moments of strength and defiance. The novel becomes a testament to the indomitable spirit of women navigating a world in flux.

Women holds a distinctive place in the canon of Polish literature. Nałkowska's prose is both evocative and incisive, capturing the nuances of emotion and social critique with equal prowess. The novel's enduring relevance lies in its ability to transcend its historical context, resonating with contemporary readers grappling with questions of gender equality and societal expectations.

---

[1] Urszula Chowaniec, *Women's Voices and Feminism in Polish Cultural Memory* (Newcastle-upon-Tyne: Cambridge Scholars Publishing, 2013), 26-46.

A Guide to Pronunciation

These are aproximate pronunciations of names and place names in the text. Use the link to hear the proper pronuciations. www.youtube.com/watch?v=0wH6-xbx8EI

Andrzej	[ahn-JAY]
Czołhański	[chōw-HINE-skee]
Dernowicz	[dare-NO-veetch]
Imszańska*	[eem-SHINE-skah]
Imszański	[eem-SHINE-skee]
Janina	[yah-NEE-nah]
Janka	[YAWN-kah]
Janusz	[YAWN-oosh]
Jerzy	[YEAH-zheh]
Jędruś	[YEN-droosh]
Łódź	[WOOJ]
Józef	[YOU-zeff]
Nierwiska	[nyer-VEE-skah]
Obojański	[oh-boy-INE-skee]
Owiński	[oh-VEEN-skee]
Pani†	[PAW-nee]
Radłowski	[rahd-WHOAFF-skee]
Rosławski	[roh-SWAFF-skee]
Sedniewska	[sed-NYEFF-skah]
Śmiłowicz	[shmee-WHOA-veetch]
Wiążewski	[vyawn-ZHEFF-skee]
Witold	[VEE-told]

* The different endings of the husbands' and wives' names is a linguistic convention in Polish due to grammatical gender. So, a husband will have the last name "Imszański," but his wife's and his daughter's last name will be "Imszańska." Often, Poles will say simply "Imszański" to mean "Mr. Imszański," and "Imszańska" to mean "Mrs. Imszańska."

† "Pani" is Polish for "Miss," "Mrs.," and even "Ms." In a few places in the text I have opted for Pani when coming before a first name instead Madame as it appears before surnames. In Polish, one commonly uses Pani before the first name of a woman one is acquainted with.

I
THE PLAINS OF ICE

Wrapped in a belt of morning-glory and vetches in full bloom, and adorning my head with a large wreath of robust corn-flowers, I recline on my back in the clearing of the forest.

It's a beautiful summer afternoon, and the air is heavy with warmth. Up in the pines, there's a faint, continuous murmur, a touch melancholic; the birches, with their slender swaying branches, emit a soft whisper, yet there's no breeze to be felt.

As I lay here, I soon start humming a melodic chant—not a familiar tune, but a composition of various melodies, some heard long ago or perhaps never heard at all. The lyrics, too, are either recollections or spontaneously generated as I sing. If the rhyme eludes me, I don't interrupt the melody to find one but let an assonance suffice. Thus, I sing of a dream I've dreamt, and then of love—intense, fervent love—and I conclude with an invocation to the woodland Faun, for my longing is directed towards him.

The atmosphere is warm and tranquil. Occasionally, birds chirp in fits and starts—so hushed that they appear to be whispering. I half anticipate glimpsing an antelope, its long horns curving back from its brow, peering out longingly between the birch trunks.

The sun, casting twinkling patterns of light onto the pine needles as they quiver, produces mobile, sparkling circles. I shut my eyes. A large, bright stain emerges, followed by a succession of rainbow hues, concluding with a spot of vivid scarlet flame.

It's warm and quiet. The fragrance of wild thyme fills my nostrils. Picture me, a woodland nymph, anticipating the arrival of the Faun of the woods!

I've left behind my vast plains of ice, my Northern Lights, and my cold silvery dreams among the stalactites of my grottoes. I've come to revel in the radiant sunshine of life.

On the remnants of my mystical dreams, a luxuriant and thriving flower has emerged—the adoration of Life and its pleasures. My resignation is wholehearted and regally complete, for I do love life despite everything.

My mind, that cruel, insatiable, and gloomy entity, would have annihilated happiness, but I now suppress it. Today, I shall seize the vibrant, flame-red blossom of Life, and my song shall summon the Faun!

No Faun answers my call; instead of his hooves, I discern the distant gallop of a horse. Placing my ear to the ground, I confirm it.

Indeed, I recognize it: Janusz is approaching. I cease my singing and lie still; he rides along the forest path. I hope he might overlook me, concealed among the pines. Yet, I'm not oblivious to the fact that if he were to pass without spotting me, I would feel a twinge of disappointment. Nonetheless, I remain motionless. The only deception I aim to avoid is self-deception.

Janusz, spotting me from a distance among the birches and pines, urges his horse forward and approaches from behind so that I cannot see him. It seems he intends to surprise me, perhaps startle or unnerve me to throw me off balance. Consequently, I make a deliberate effort not to move, lying with my hands clasped beneath my head, gazing up at the sky.

He charges toward me, reining in his horse just two paces away. Immediately, he senses that my posture is a challenge, and it vexes him. There's a moment of silence. To make me turn my head, he keeps his horse in the same spot—a challenging feat.

I, however, remain still, suppressing a desire to laugh. Janusz is too skilled a rider to allow his horse to trample on me. I hear the horse snorting impatiently, its hooves pawing the ground.

Tormented by the flies in the woods, the horse eventually can't contain itself and moves a few paces forward, bringing Janusz into view. He is a handsome man, wearing a light-colored jockey's cap, tight-fitting trousers, and long patent leather boots. At this moment, he's visibly irritated, with quivering nostrils.

With a stiff bow, he takes his right foot out of the stirrup, preparing to dismount.

"I thought you might not have seen me and continued riding," I casually remark with a faint, disinterested smile.

"As it turns out, I didn't miss you."

"So, I see."

"Did you want me to miss you?"

"I did."

"For what reason, pray?"

"I was in a very pleasant mood—a sort of pantheistic communion with nature that requires solitude to be enjoyed."

"Nevertheless, I am going to stay," he asserts determinedly, carefully tying his horse's reins to a pine branch.

A brief silence ensues. Janusz brushes a few pine cones out of his way and then settles beside me. I sit up, adjust the wreath of cornflowers on my head, and lean against a tree trunk.

"Can't you see that we are not in harmony?" he asks after a while.

"That may very well be," I respond with some disdain. "And how did you manage to find me?"

"I followed you."

"Indeed?"

"My balcony offers a sweeping view. Your rose-colored dress was quite visible as you strolled through the meadows and fields. You followed the path along the ditch, didn't you? And then into the woods, where you vanished. I pursued on horseback along the highroad, a much shorter route."

"Yes, your more direct route, though less picturesque than mine."

"Am I meant to discern a hidden meaning in this?"

"Oh, no, feel free to interpret it as you wish."

Janusz is one who enjoys "intellectual" conversation. I employ all the social tact I possess, striving to engage him at his level. I seek to captivate him not solely with my physical appearance but with the allure of my intellect, now harnessed in service of my physical self. My coquetry adapts to the psychical character of its target, guided by the Law of Contrast. For instance, when I initially flirted with Rosławski, I emphasized the primal, elemental aspects of my nature, only to later alter my approach. Acting upon Janusz, I leverage my womanly wisdom, wit, and originality; even if I were to lose some of my physical attractiveness, I would still be equally lovable in his eyes. In the contemporary psychology of love, this holds significant weight.

A fleeting glow passes over his handsome, well-defined face. His eyes are fixed on my features. Meanwhile, I, swift in change like a chameleon, adorned with radiant looks and glances, observe him with artistic and entirely impersonal interest. With his quivering, sensitive nostrils, he resembles a beautiful, high-bred animal. His usually beaming and glistening eyes are now dimmed and glazed, as if the fire within him has been extinguished by passion. Occasionally, his eyes lower before mine, and he attempts to summon a pleasant smile, though in doing so, his white teeth gleam dangerously.

A gnat settles on his forehead, and I point it out to him. He waves it away nonchalantly.

"Let it bite," he says with a smile, "it matters little. I have plenty of blood to spare."

There's a touch of self-satisfaction in his voice as he speaks. It was a mistake on my part to assume he was unaware of the nature of his strength. Knowledge of one's strong points contributes to happiness; he is indeed enviable.

Now, he picks up some pine cones and playfully pelts his horse with them. The horse starts to kick and stamp. Instead of needlessly teasing the poor creature, I suggest he pick one of the trees as a target. With that, I approach the horse. It gives me a distrustful look out of its beautiful eyes while I stroke and pat its neck.

"Miss Janina, do not get so close to my beast; it may hurt you."

"You weren't afraid when it was just now standing close to my head," I reply with a laugh.

"But I was holding it in then," he mutters between his clenched teeth.

He advances towards me, extending his hand to pull me away forcefully, but a quick glance of surprise from me instantly subdues him.

"I beg you," he says in a voice half-strangled with emotion, "I beg you to let me kiss your hand."

He is very close to me. For a moment, I am as hot as fire, but I don't draw away or place my hands behind me. Standing still, with my head half-averted and bent down close to the horse's mane, I calmly reply:

"I will not."

Janusz, with a dog-like obedience, steps back and stands a few paces away.

"Let's go home now," I say after a brief silence, "but you must let me ride your horse."

"With the utmost pleasure, but then how will you manage without a saddle fit for you?"

"Oh, that's alright. Even on your saddle, I can manage to ride in a ladylike manner. You just have to adjust the stirrup."

I spring into the saddle, my foot just brushing against his hand. Janusz himself adjusts the stirrup, shortening it for me, and I notice a glow sweep over his face as he does so.

"Please allow me to lead the horse. It's restless and might throw you," he suggests.

"No, thanks; I'm not afraid at all."

Suddenly, with an unexpected movement, he seizes me and presses his face against my knees. Almost simultaneously, I give the horse a sharp blow with my whip, galloping away without looking back. It's not easy to maintain balance on that saddle.

I haven't done this to escape from him or out of fear. It's simply to prevent him from noticing my flushed face, which is neither flushed with indignation nor shame.

Janusz has gone to L. for a few days. I'm alone with Marta, with whom I find great enjoyment. There's no one else on earth with whom I can share the pleasure of reading wise and beautiful books together. As we read, we get lost in mutual admiration for the depth and subtlety of our remarks, leading to a delightful state of mind in which each loses awareness of the other's presence. Our impressions are instantaneous and immediate; a look or gesture is enough for one to understand the other. We are growing remarkably similar, almost identical. Isolated from our surroundings, our minds converge on dizzying heights, bridged by ethereal connections that bring our souls together over the tremendous gulfs beneath us. In the valleys of the mind, it's not difficult for two souls to unite. However, as one reaches the mountain peaks, they become increasingly distant, and the chasm between them deepens. Moreover, with the tread of the first heavy foot, those finely crafted bridges, spanning from peak to peak, break and fall apart.

There is no love, nor any affection, lost between Marta and me; we don't even refer to each other as friends. We share the belief that true love is impossible between women, and we don't attempt to deceive ourselves with a facsimile. Even though we don't openly express everything in words, we possess an uncanny understanding of each other.

The one thing that could strain our connection is if we were rivals for a man's affection. Fortunately, Marta deems this scenario highly unlikely. She tends toward asceticism and takes pride in the fact that no one has ever loved her. She typically enjoys portraying herself as someone misunderstood and underappreciated by the world and men. This role suits her well, given her attractive appearance, and no one takes it too seriously.

"My life," she often declares, "is as pure as a blank page; no thrill is recorded there, no kiss, no blush. I have no faith except in the crystal transparency of my being, in the knowledge that Life passes close to me, touches me, grazes me, and yet, by some miracle, never leaves a single streak of golden pollen from the flowers she bears on my long white robe. My only faith, the only thing I care about, is the conviction that I will go through life nobly and beautifully, in infinite sweetness and tranquility; that my journey on earth will be filled with sunshine and loveliness, like the blossoming of a rare and splendid flower. So may I die! Even if love could bring me happiness, I would still keep my distance from it."

Yes, but occasionally, in the dim blue twilight, Marta plays Grieg's "Der Frühling," and then I sense that what she says is not entirely true. In her notes, there is an unspeakable tone of longing that softly pleads for something. Her fair white soul always seems to be sobbing with pain and perpetually dreaming—always dreaming—of love.

After all is said and done, I am clever, young, and attractive, so I want to live my life. Nietzsche insists that we not forget the law: "For a woman, a stick." Amiel contends that she must love only one and adhere to a sexual morality tailored exclusively for her.[1] Garborg suggests she should not go anywhere without a governess, ensuring her future husband finds suspicion impossible.[2] Despite all of this, I am determined to live my own woman's life.

So far, I haven't figured out what femininity fundamentally is. During the Rosławski period, I devoutly believed that aesthetic feeling was the paramount characteristic of womanliness. But now—Ellen Key[3] posits that a woman always shapes herself as the man desires. If he, the Only One, is a primitive, domineering, despotic man, am I supposed to flavor his siesta and cigar with witty conversation, bind my hair, dance, and sound the timbrel for him, while revealing only my eyes to others, keeping my face hidden under a veil? I just want to live my woman's life... nothing more. Until, perhaps...

Oh, how difficult it is for a girl to bear the weight of conscious humanity on her white and shapely shoulders!

At times, Janusz is as gentle as a tame young wolf, and the ravenous look fades from his eyes. Then I allow him to kiss my hands and press them to his sunburnt cheeks. When the wild beast within him falls asleep for a while, he exhibits all the kindness and sweetness of a child. Yet, even then, I sense the presence of a latent force that may erupt at any moment—an inexplicable force that appears antagonistic to me.

"How I wish you would allow me to call you my darling!" he exclaimed today while sitting at my feet on a turf bank, gently touching the border of my skirt like a favorite cat.

Looking down at the long lashes of his downcast eyes, his scarlet lips, and his beautifully chiseled nose, I thought to myself, "Why don't you then? I would only press one long, loving kiss—perhaps two—upon those lips of yours and leave you without a single word of regret."

"Are you offended then?" he asked, looking up at me.

I knitted my brows slightly, but the corners of my mouth couldn't stay still.

"Yes, I am."

"But you're smiling. Why do you smile so strangely?"

And his eyes gazed at me from under his thick brows—gazed slyly and sweetly, while the hot blood burned in my cheeks. Never, in the days of Rosławski and our long, learned conversations about literature, did I feel such a sensation as this.

An evening party at the Sedniewskis in Topolów, celebrating somebody's name-day. All four of us attend—Marta and I, the grandfather, and Janusz. It's a sizable gathering, with girls like flowers, fresh and brightly hued. Some young men have been brought in for the occasion from as far as Łódź.

Entering with my cheeks fresh and ruddy from our windy drive, dressed in a beautiful sea-green hue, I make the usual impression. For a while, as every glance is turned in my direction, I feel as if pitted against them all. However, despite not knowing many people here, I am not embarrassed even for a moment. The unfriendly atmosphere around me and the sense of my loneliness in this crowd only fuel a reaction of haughty defiance. I would feel more awkward if I didn't make this impression and entered without attracting any attention at all.

As Madame Sedniewska welcomes me, I catch a whispered remark on my left: "Dressed like a third-rate actress."

This piques my interest, and I turn around, thinking the observation, though off the mark, is rather neatly expressed. A tall girl, dressed in white English style from head to foot, meets my eyes and silently exchanges glances with me. Without a doubt, it's her. After all the introductions have been made, I choose to engage in conversation with her.

Her name is Imszańska; she has an unattractive fiancé and a handsome brother, the most interesting of all the young men present, in my opinion. He politely asks how I like the countryside here and then continues talking to Marta, who, in her evening dress, looks less comely than usual, her face pale and wearing an expression of unnatural constraint.

We have tea, after which the dancing begins.

Dancing is as enjoyable to me as riding, and I am an excellent dancer. In one of the long mirrors that reach to the floor, I repeatedly catch sight of myself and the black arms encircling me, my listless form thrown back indolently, almost sleepily, my red lips contrasting with the white of my set teeth, and sea-green gauze floating around me in loose watery undulations. The elastic, snake-like stalks of great white water lilly blossoms twine around my figure.

It becomes evident that I have made an impression—so palpable that the women themselves pretend to be not only unconcerned but pleased at my success. One of them is kind enough to straighten a hairpin for me. In such gatherings, the competition to be first, while robbing it of some of the pleasure it should directly provide, offers the interest of a game where the harder it is to win, the more intoxicating the victory becomes.

After the cotillion, which I danced with Imszański, I partner with Janusz for the "Oberek." He is a perfect master of ceremonies, and as such, he is *sans peur et sans reproche*.[4]

I prefer dancing with him above all. He propels me forward like a runaway steed. Spiraling in a tiny orbit, leaning towards the center all the while, we turn round and round with vertiginous speed, like two planets gone mad. Locked in each other's arms, propelled by our own momentum, we glide along with half-closed eyes, involuntarily and almost unconsciously, with a passive motion, as if unable to keep up with such a tremendous pace by ourselves. Around us, only a confused mass of thick, clotted brightness is perceivable; the lights, mirrors, and the brilliant circle of onlookers are no longer distinguishable as they fly around us, all merging into one maze of colors.

A wild flame is gleaming in my partner's eyes, and their pupils are sparkling like sunlit diamonds. Our maddening pace, combined with the boisterous, musically monotonous din of the dance tune, affects him like a war dance on a primitive race.

As for me, despite his hot breath on me like a flame, I feel quite calm. Tired out, almost fainting, I meekly let his wild "ravishing strides" carry me along as he chooses.

Finally, I return to my seat; a deafening thunder of applause greets us both. I bow my head to thank them, but for some time, I can distinguish nothing. Meanwhile, I hear Janusz, who has regained his self-control, ordering the orchestra to play the "Mazur."[5]

Miss Imszańska, coming up and sitting beside me, says, "You dance with all the grace of a swan; my brother says he never saw anything like it."

In the intervals between dances, we stroll in the extensive, tree-filled garden. The white flowers of the tobacco plants, just visible at night against the blackness of the yard, emit their strange and intense aroma. A kind of drowsy hallucination takes hold of me: I imagine I am no longer on earth but in some Hades of flowers, sweet sounds, beautiful things, and Night triumphant. I lean heavily on Janusz, almost nestling in his arms. My smile gleams white in the dusk, and my long eyelashes quiver as if with sleep. Janusz bends over me, and his gaze seeks to meet mine.

"Look at me!" he whispers, glowing with impatience.

I too am all aglow; yet I turn my head away and stubbornly look at some cluster of bushes in the distance. But all the while, my heart beseeches him, repeating over and over: "Kiss me, kiss me—now—now—now!"

A moment ago, a dress was still looming in the dark in front of us; now we are quite alone. Our eyes have begun to make out the shapes of things; we can discern the trees and the long, narrow strip of pathway where we are walking between two hedges of the thicket. Black cloud-like shadows seem to flee away now, then gather and close upon us.

Suddenly, a spasm of horrible, unearthly dread clutches at my heart.

"Good God! Look there!" I cry.

"What—what of it?"

I raise my hand to my eyes, shudder all over with fear, and press close to him.

"There—just beneath us, far, horribly far down—there is water!"

"Well, what of that? There is nothing to be frightened of. I know the garden; it is only a brook that feeds the pond."

"Let's go away—away at once. I saw it glitter through the leaves in the dark: it was so strange! And so deep down—an abyss where I never dreamed the ground sloped at all."

"But we could not fall in: there is a stone barrier."

"No matter," I whisper, half-frantic with dread. "Let's go!"

We make our way back. Janusz is silent, but I feel, as I am holding to his arm, that he too is trembling. He might have comforted me with the words: "Fear nothing by my side!" For just a minute ago, I had boundless confidence in him. Now I know that he can be frightened.

We hear the sounds of the harp and the violin, and a row of lit windows shines on the pitch-black trees.

Janusz breaks the silence. "I have no fear in a forest at night; I fear neither robbers nor wild beasts: but things one cannot explain are not to my liking."

Yes, I quite understand, and share the same dislike: but somehow, I had a fancy that...

We dance merrily until morning; my painful impression has quite faded.

As we return, we change places; Marta goes with her grandfather, and I am with Janusz. Daybreak reveals a lovely landscape: hills covered with dark woods, fields white with stubble. The sky grows rosy, and we catch ever new glimpses of dim heights, solitary pear-trees scattered in the fields, and tall, somber poplars in rows, marking the highways in the plain.

We travel along a road full of deep holes, climbing heights and descending into valleys. The enchanting beauty of the surrounding countryside captivates us.

As the sun rises, it casts distinct, mobile shadows on the road, lengthening our two carriages and our figures monstrously. I feel stupefied after a sleepless night, my face hot, and my lips burning. Despite the plaid and rugs, I shiver with cold. I close my eyes and lean my head against the back of the carriage, listening to the screaking wheels, the trot of the snorting horses, and the timid chirruping of the birds just roused by daylight. Though awake, I am in a dreamlike state.

Janusz bends over me, touching my lips with his in a gentle kiss, as if trying not to wake me. I remain motionless, pretending to sleep, well aware that Janusz knows I am awake. And now my golden morning has arrived!

On one of the last warm summer days, Marta and I bathe together outside the park. When undressed, she is very pleasant to look upon. She pretends to object but puts on her bathing dress so deliberately that I can gaze at my ease. After bathing in the clear cool water, we return and lie down on the lush grass in the park, surrounded by tall trunks bare to a great height. Far above us, their branches form a canopy of bright green under the blue sky.

"I wonder," I say to her, "how plain people feel about themselves. With us, comeliness is such a matter of course! If I were to lose my good looks, or even my knowledge that I am good-looking, I really think I could not bear life. It is that alone which gives me strength in the presence of others. I go out in the full glare of day without a parasol; in company, I sit with my face turned straight to the lamplight; I walk in the crowd with head erect, fearing no one, abashed by no one—simply because I know that the sight of me must cause pleasure. If I am good-natured, it is because of my good looks. I hate nobody, envy nobody, and am filled with a sort of Pagan, sunlit, royal love for all."

"And which of us two do you think is prettier?" asks Marta.

"I don't know. In reality, each of us thinks herself prettier, but we are both too cultured ever to have tried to make conclusions on that subject."

Strictly speaking, I am not as fair as she; however, I possess a certain grace that she lacks. Besides, my eyes have a golden tint, a uniqueness that sets me apart from other girls, as far as I can tell.

I often walk a few versts[6] with Marta, heading to the "Kirkut," or Jewish cemetery. There, hewn gravestones stand in long, parallel rows adorned with cabalistic signs and symbols, such as a lion, a broken taper, or a shelf of books. The graves, covered in moss, heather, and wild thyme, almost blend with the ground. The wooden enclosure, over which we always climb, disappears into the woods among pine trunks. Those long, regular rows of stones seem to rise in a forest untouched by man. Here, I feel as though I've stepped far back into the dim immemorial past.

I love that burial ground; I love contemplating Life triumphing over Death. As I gaze, I lose my fear of Death. Death takes only the individual, the accidental manifestations of Life; Life itself endures. I see myself standing for all of mankind, identified with Life. I always existed, and I'll be eternal. Death is peacefully slumbering beneath my feet.

With that, a delightful sense of infinite might overcomes me. I find no limit to my power and continuity. I am not of the earth, not Janka Dernowicz; I am eternal, unsleeping consciousness; I am the Universe! In this burial ground, Janusz becomes dismal, talking about the transience of all earthly things—a beautiful creature living in fear of Death!

What if it were true that animals have no souls?

At times, I feel unjustified longings for the man who entered and exited my life like a hurricane. Yes, now and again, I yearn for my plains of ice and Northern Lights!

Once he asked if I would never wish to feel, think, and strive along with a companion in life.

I burst into laughter then, hating sentiment and the blending of love with a "brotherhood of souls."

Now, I'm near thinking that this man, whom I never loved, might be the only one fit to become my husband. Often at night, lying awake and staring into the darkness with wide-open eyes, I feel burning lips, lips famished with hunger, pressed to mine.

And when I seize the kiss upon those lips, I know that they are the lips, not of Rosławski, but of Janusz.

And then I am full of terror, fearing that an irreversible evil has been done—lest something may have fallen away forever out of my life. Then, I no longer feel any desire for anyone, and I weep in the dark, silently, not to awaken Marta.

In the morning, I look upon Janusz with hatred and loathing, treating him harshly, though he is not to blame. I use him ill because my soul is wandering alone over those plains of ice of mine, still dreaming cold silvery dreams, seeking in vain for a fraternal soul.

Is it then impossible to be in love without also loving?

While out shooting today, Janusz had the same gleam in his eyes as when he looks at me. He is a typical primitive man of a nomad race of hunters, in whom the instinct of conservation manifests itself vehemently when procuring his own subsistence as well as for the preservation of the race. Game is a vital necessity; so is a woman.

I felt sorry for the hares he had killed and lectured him on man's cruelty in taking the lives of defenseless, innocent creatures. Just now, I was thinking how I'd like to lock Janusz up in a nice cage, having him all to myself. I'd give him plenty of food but neither let him read (that prohibition he wouldn't find very hard) nor talk to anyone so that, with all his vitality, he might be mine alone. And occasionally, I'd enter the cage.

I'd be far more spiritually disposed than I am now. Currently, my splendid, primitive, untamed beast is hungry and howling, marring the divine symphony I listen to in my dreams of light.

I should appease it and walk in my sacred grove along the margin of the dark abysmal lake within my soul. And I would willingly have Rosławski to walk with me there!

Janusz has asked me if I would consent to become his wife.

"If only for a month or two, I would with pleasure," was my truthful reply, which I later turned into a jest: not a nice one, I must say.

Janusz darted one or two angry looks at me and gave vent to this aphorism: "There are things one should never jest about."

Most certainly he is right. And all this begins to worry me just a little.

I might perhaps fancy myself playing the part of his seductress; as his wife, never. And what to do with him now, I can't tell.

I should like to go away now. Oh, why has all this come about so suddenly?

Out boating late in the evening, on the great pond beyond the park.

I have consented to come here, for I am so wretched, I want to die. And I know that Janusz, whom I have been tormenting all day long, can no longer control himself.

His nerves are racked to the very utmost; it is my doing. He clutches me by the shoulders and holds me down to the side of the boat with an iron grip. To get the better of his mad fit, I keep myself very passive and cool.

"Hear me, Janka!" he growls between his teeth, his face close to mine, "you! listen: I am speaking for the last time. Say Yes!"

I could disarm him with a single cry of pain or fear: but I remain mute. I must have strong sensations tonight.

"I'll kill—I'll kill you! Do you hear? I hate you as much as I love you, and more. Speak instantly—speak!"

His rage is suffocating him; the words stick in his throat. His knee is pressed hard upon my bosom; his nails dig deep into my flesh. With all my strength, I stifle a groan and wait. The boat is careening over more and more, beginning to be waterlogged.

"I shall drown you! See, the boat is about to go down! Say Yes!"

Gently and quietly, I gaze into his untamed, fiery eyes, where the whites gleam through the surrounding darkness and captivate me.

In a fleeting moment, a desire creeps in to shut my eyelids and fade away, slipping silently into the inky water. Despite that impulse, my eyes instinctively lock onto his.

Abruptly, I sense the weakening grip of his clenched hands.

Now confident of triumph, I whisper, "No!" with a subtle smile.

Janusz, releasing a cry of anguish, retreats into the boat. He fervently presses his forehead against my feet, showering them with kisses, overcome by convulsive sobs. The boat regains its stability, rocking tumultuously.

However, I find no joy in my victory. Doubt clouds my belief in the sheer might of physical strength, overshadowed by the potency of the mind.

If Janusz had persisted in grappling with me for a few more seconds, I might have yielded. Now, I envy the unparalleled joy he would have experienced in acknowledging my dominance.

A true warrior takes delight not in conquering the weaker but in admitting the power of the one who proves stronger and overcomes him.

Observing this contorted figure, shaking with sobs that gradually fade with fatigue, I gaze far into the night. No moon, no stars. The rushes along the shore maintain a constant rustle.

And the dark lake, a reflection of my soul, stares upward with unseeing eyes at the somber sky.

All is lifeless: no signs of life anywhere. All that remains is my loneliness—boundless, self-centered, and unparalleled in strength.

Never before have I felt my power so intensely, and never before has it left me so melancholic.

The black sky arches menacingly above me; beneath its clouds, the dark pond churns with swelling waves. In the vast expanse between the Infinite and my soul, there is no room for strength.

Oh, "I am so weary, weary of these heights!" How I long to encounter a force capable of subduing my own!

"Please, Janusz, rise," I implore, gently stroking his hair. "It must be very late. Where are the oars?"

Lying in the hollow between two rows of graves, I inhale the fragrance of white forest carnations blooming in the "Kirkut," contemplating life—the most admirable and beautiful marvel. I share with Marta the philosophy that my reverence for life stems from resignation.

"Yet, in me, resignation has taken a form different from yours. The creed of despairing pride, 'If I cannot have all, I refuse to have anything,' is embraced by slaves and wretched men. My belief in Azoism is the creed of a proud woman reconciled to her slavery, rejecting spurious imitations of freedom.[7] This withdrawal from the vortex, allowing me to view all things from above with a smile of dignified amenity, is what I cherish. I often feel so ill-suited for life on Earth that it seems I've wandered here by mistake, a blunder."

Marta responds, "Adaptation to the environment benefits only brute animals; man can create his own world by perceiving it in his unique way."

Sadly, she adds, "I believe in nothing. Yet, women, in general, tend to have faith in an existence after death—a result of sympathy with suffering and an instinct for justice. Useless suffering in nature drives me to madness. Consider the silent agonies unknown, the tortures endured by multitudes worldwide leaving no trace behind them. When Janusz, as a little boy, focused the sun's rays on a wing-fastened insect writhing in impotent throes, I still see those poor limbs, red in the glow, quivering in excruciating pain until I snatched the lens away, setting the half-roasted creature free. Those were its last impressions of life, followed by nothingness. I trample hundreds of tiny invisible beings in my daily walks, leaving them to expire in dreadful torments under pine needles. I know the pain fish endure, often kept alive in the air for days, convulsing even on the fire. All this pain, with nothing to justify or compensate for it! Beyond death, there is nothing!"

"But did it never occur to you that if there is nothing beyond death, it's impossible for 'nothingness' to be there?"

She looks at me inquisitively.

"The concepts of justice, vengeance, and compensation are purely earthly, once forming a religious ideal in the worship of Jehovah. I place them in the same category as the concept of mercy prevailing among Christians. Some other idea will emerge later, equally foreign to the notion of existence beyond the grave."

"Well, and what do you infer from that?"

"My belief is that the phenomenon called death consists in our losing all sensations, categories, concepts, and all projections of this world, and in finding other sensations in the next. Perhaps not even that. In the next world, just as there will be no idea of justice, there may be none of sensations. Do you follow me?"

"So, you think you shall continue to exist then?"

"I cannot say—I cannot say."

For a few minutes, I listen to the undertone of the pine trees sounding far above us in the sky.

"You see," I continue, "there, it may well be, we shall have no idea of an Ego that excludes and contradicts the non-Ego. The distinction between them has arisen from our existence on Earth: it is a form into which we mold our impressions; something purely accidental, depending upon the quality and mechanism of the brain. There, too, the idea of Time may be wanting; also, that of Space. Of course, from our earthly point of view, it is nonsense to say that the world is boundless: that which the brain calls 'the Infinite' cannot be represented in imagination as space. Truly, there are times when I simply feel admiration for a God who has created so great and endlessly complicated a scheme of beings."

Marta's disappointment is plain to perceive.

"So, then you believe in God?"

"I don't know, and don't trouble with it. It's not likely the ideas of creation out of nothing, of sovereignty as opposed to subjection, of volition as opposed to passiveness, have any counterpart out of our minds. Notice, Marta, that in my view, the expression 'Transcendental Being' implies a contradiction. Our very idea of Being is a mere outcome of experience: and I go so far beyond Nature, I leap so completely out of my human skin, that I can force myself to the contemplation of an unimaginable world in which there is no contradiction between Being and non-Being.

"Therefore, I don't worry whether I shall in that world be myself or not myself: nor even whether I shall be or not be."

She gazes at me, her eyes wide open, and says under her breath:

"Yes, I see."

"And, do you know, the capacity of thus abstracting one's thought itself from its outward form, of looking upon the universe and one's very thought from such a standpoint, sets one on heights incomprehensibly sublime, and gives the purest, the most unearthly delight."

There is a black cat here, with eyes like emeralds; it prowls noiselessly amongst the rows of gravestones. A singularly sociable creature; it follows us everywhere in our walks, like a dog. When I look at it, I cannot help believing in Metempsychosis: there must dwell within this cat some very refined aristocratic soul, one that looks upon everything with supreme skepticism.

"What's wrong, Marta?"

"Nothing. I've just dropped a hairpin."

A tortoiseshell pin has fallen out of her thick black tresses, dropping onto the earth with a faint sound.

Marta is in a very lofty mood. This real world strikes her as a contrast, ridiculous in its smallness, to the world we are speaking of. So, she does not wish me to pick up that pin, though it has dropped quite close to me on the heather. To my mind, this is too high-flown, too girlish. After all, the realities of life are paramount, and we ought to have so much intellectual culture as never to forget it.

Therefore, I give her the pin, smiling very sarcastically.

"After all," I conclude, rising from the hollow ridge and preparing to walk home, "I quite understand that what I've said amounts to the same as believing in nothing. It's all the same to me whether I shall cease to be after death or be transferred to a world wherein there is no idea of being or of any Ego conditioning my self-consciousness. I understand, too, that a world in which Being does not contradict non-Being is, to our minds, equivalent to no world at all. So that my faith is similar to your unfaith but inferred and formulated otherwise."

Janusz is currently very humble and wretched. Sometimes, during our long evening sits together, he falls asleep with his head in my lap, worn out from nervous exhaustion. In those moments, I confront something very strange.

I feel a mysterious dread of the torment of an everlasting vigil, coupled with a sense of responsibility beyond my strength. Despite my shuddering dread, I resist waking him, refusing to let him know that I am afraid. Certain things are better left unsaid, especially to those we care for. I keep hidden the fact that I love solitude when alone, but the feeling of solitude when someone is by my side fills me with unspeakable dread. In those moments, I hear my soul uttering her triumphant laugh, a revelation I would never confess to him.

I am vigorous and capable of struggling for a long time. Yet, even warriors have moments when they trustingly lay their tired heads on someone's lap, feeling secure in the knowledge of someone above them watching over them, standing between them and their foes, between them and the Infinite, the Unknown.

Is there any man in the world who could lull my watchfulness to sleep? There is one, only one. But the price I would pay would be everything that makes life charming.

When Janusz is sleeping on my lap, I invariably think of—Rosławski.

Typically, I view whatever happens in my life from a novelist's or an artist's standpoint—from without and objectively. I consciously throw all my impressions into the form of sentences, rounded and complete, often affected, and unnatural. In everything I say, think, or do, I seek dramatic, literary, or picturesque effects. I consider this peculiarity one of the tragic aspects of my life since it almost entirely robs my impressions of their directness.

Some people blame me for being mannered, for posing, for performing everything with artifice, whether making a bow or styling my hair. I fully admit they are right. However, artificiality comes naturally to me. Every motion, every smile of mine is preconceived, scrutinized, and judged by me as though I were someone else. There is no present for me; I look at all things from the perspective of the future. There are no involuntary bursts of thought, no inarticulate words, or mechanical gestures for me. If I were to attempt apparent artlessness, it would be artificial twice over.

This afternoon, a mud-covered carriage drawn by a pair of splendid sorrel horses arrives at our terrace. Imszański jumps out, leaving the reins to the groom seated behind. Janusz welcomes him, and he slowly ascends the steps, having driven thirty-five miles with no apparent fatigue on his impassive features.

Upon closer inspection, he surpasses expectations. Undoubtedly, he is the most handsome man I know, a significant point in his favor. His movements, marked by a graceful stillness, reveal his noble descent. Bright eyes exhibit continuous concentrated thought and a tranquil, half-forgotten sorrow. He possesses every accomplishment, speaking interestingly and elegantly, with literary turns and expressions. He has a variety of smiles at his disposal but never laughs outright; considerate restraint is his specialty.

His first words upon entering are, "My sister sends you her greetings; she wanted to come with me, but I was afraid to take her. It is such a long journey, and the roads are in such bad condition now."

He courteously pays equal attention to Marta and me, being more serious with her and more gallant with me, considering I am a visitor in the neighborhood. I am nearly enchanted, and my eyes remain fixed on him. Yet, simultaneously, I realize that this paragon of a man could never succeed in winning my love. Physically, I care even less for him than for Rosławski. This indifference seems to arise from his marvelous beauty, which may divert my attention from him as a man and an intelligent being. I could gaze with the same enthusiasm at his portrait.

We venture out to inspect new varieties of ornamental shrubs recently planted in the park by Marta. Janusz walks with me, while Imszański accompanies Marta a few paces ahead. The two create a picturesque scene reminiscent of the days of old, evoking images of knights and their lady-loves in this grand old park. I notice that Marta possesses a style and breeding that I lack. To help her over a splash of water, Imszański offers his hand, and she gathers up her dress, revealing her neat and shapely ankles. They resemble dancers in a minuet, so handsome that I can't find it in my heart to envy them.

Janusz walks by my side like a shadow, and his eyes blaze as he follows my glances.

"A fine man, Imszański. You like him, don't you?" he asks. "But," he continues, "I don't advise you to try your hand at him; he belongs to another. He has loved long and hopelessly."

"Has he?"

"While in Warsaw, he went as far as attempting suicide—unsuccessfully, needless to say."

"But this love of his, is it not only hopeless, but unrequited too?"

"Well, he proposed—and was refused. But that's no wonder. Such a man should never marry; a whole haram would not be enough for him."

"H'm, yes; that would be quite in his line. Who is the girl? Does she live near?"

"Yes, she does."

"And who may she be? Please tell me. Was she at the Sedniewski party?"

"Don't ask; I musn't tell. It has been kept secret."

"But did anybody confide in you?"

"Why, no."

"Then I have as much right to know as you have. I am awfully curious, and wonder at the girl's taste. Do I know her?"

He holds out for some time, but in the end, I disarm him, though in a way I dislike most and very seldom employ, by wheedling and coaxing him. The secret shall go down to the grave with me, I promise him. He hesitates for a while, then says in an undertone:

"Marta."

I do my best to conceal my unbounded astonishment under some commonplace expressions of faint surprise. I obviously have not the slightest intention to keep my word: I will ask Marta about the whole business. Can she possibly not be in love with such a Phoenix? Can she too have found him undesirable because of that beauty of his?

During supper, I watch her closely, and see in her face that very same pallor, that very look of weariness and constraint that she was wearing in Topolów. No, his love is certainly not unrequited.

I have no fondness, and consequently no fellow-feeling, for the girl: but now I am more interested than before in her theory of "Azoism." I formerly thought she had taken it up as an apology for her life; now I see that her life itself compels her to profess it.

Imszański himself is always the same, courteous and languidly good-humored. He is talking with Marta's grandfather about this year's crops, and looking quite interested in the subject.

It is a cool windy autumn day. Clouds are floating close to the earth, rain is in the air, and no birds are seen. Along the woods stretch the fields, either already tilled, or covered with dingy whitish stubble. Something has gone out of my life forever: I cannot get rid of the thought.

We three are riding together over the desolate plain. Janusz rides in front of us, playing acrobatic tricks on horseback, and really performing wonderful feats of agility.

But the tide is now ebbing within me. Those tight trousers, those raw leather boots of his—I hate them, and scorn myself for having let that sort of thing ever make any impression on me; assuredly there is nothing in all this that is worthy of scorn.

Autumn has come. That is all.

We come abreast upon the muddy highway, all three strangely sick at heart. In silence we ride on.

Latterly Janusz has altered very much. His face is pale; it is the face of a man lost in troubled thought. When we are by ourselves, he scarcely ever raises his eyes to mine; and his outbursts of energy resemble the frenzy of delirium. After the equestrian evolutions just performed, he looks wearied and gloomy, and his lips are closed fast as he rides.

Why are we all like this? I alone can tell. Because Marta is thinking of Imszański, and Janusz of me, and I am thinking of Rosławski. It is just like a novel: each of us as remote as one star is from another.

I got a post-card from Obojański yesterday, saying he had come back; so, I shall have to be off in four days. I must then see Rosławski, who has no doubt returned to Warsaw by now. A fever of impatience possesses me.

On my return, I lie down on the drawing-room sofa, still in my riding-habit.

Marta, as usual, is making her way from pantry to cellar, Janusz has gone to dress for supper; "Grandfather" is probably asleep in some nook. I feel impatient at the thought of seeing Him again. I'm frustrated, tearing at my hair, sobbing silently and without tears.

My misery is overwhelming. Moreover, I feel something else: a sorrow for leaving—sorry for Janusz. There's something tearing within me, shredding my soul into bits, shreds, and tatters.

I hear Janusz coming, adopt an easy recumbent posture without rising from the sofa, and fix my hair. "What! You're here already?" I remark in a peevishly flippant tone of inquiry.

He doesn't reply but approaches with noiseless reverent steps, in an attitude of supreme worship, like an idolater to the idol he adores. Kneeling down before me, he gently takes my hands and presses them to his brow. I don't withdraw them. I lean forwards instinctively.

"Janka, listen," he says tenderly, in a voice trembling with suppressed emotion; "say that you will be my wife; say so, my dear. You know what you've made of me. You laughed at me for my sober-mindedness, my shallow outlook on life, my thoughtless *joie de vivre.* Now I'm quite different. Now I am like you and the rest of your set. Could I ever, in the old days, have thought it possible that I should become like a child—crying my eyes out at the thought of your going away, Janka? I have nothing in the world to console me but you. Janka, since you told me you were sorry for the hares I had killed, I have not gone out shooting anymore. Oh, I shall not struggle with you; I shall not be the master, but your slave, I beg you, I entreat you, be my wife! Oh, my adorable lady, my sweetest one, say but that you will! You will be happy; you will see me do everything, everything to please you. You will live like a princess. If you will not give me this assurance, I shall go to ruin, indeed I shall. Janka, I will leave the University without taking my degree. I will follow you everywhere on earth. Marta, too; does she not love you? And does it matter to you if you say Yes now? Nothing hinders you from saying the word; I even think you love me just a little. Oh, Janka, Janka!"

He ends with a burst of tears. My head bends down to his, and we both weep together. In turns, I am torn by compassion for him and by my longing for Rosławski. I kiss his black silky curls, and we cry like children.

Finally, we agree that I shall go to Warsaw "to take counsel with my family and with my own heart"; and I am to give him a definite answer in a month's time.

By then I shall surely have seen Rosławski—and everything will have been settled: for life or for death.

Every morning, the trees in the park are now white with frost, and we find the threshing-floor in the barn covered with many a steel-blue swallow, lying frozen to death. The stoves are heated, the windows hermetically sealed (for the time being), and, though autumn has but just commenced, we are in winter quarters already.

In the calm white country house, sleep reigns supreme.

The wild wind howls through the somber shrubberies, and sweeps showers of drifting leaves, green but frostbitten, along the walls of the park. Through the windows, I look out into the cold bleak night, a night of desolation and evil omen: such a night as one might expect to bring us mysterious half-frozen travelers who have lost their way; and on this very night they should come knocking at the door. The old, faithful, superstitious servants should mutter the saying: "Someone's hanged themselves, the wind's so high," and the dogs should howl together mournfully.

There is no light except in one window, from which, through the broad gaps in the shutters, its bright streaks filter out into the park. The maids are there, keeping vigil as usual; Janusz and the old man have gone to bed and have long been asleep.

Around there breathes that stillness and quiet sense of security which a winter night often brings—an atmosphere of repose.

I am kneeling by the fire, in a plain dressing-gown, with my hands clasped behind my head, and my eyes fixed upon the flames. Flashes of red light up my dark face and my chestnut hair. Now and then, I put big logs on the fire from the heap close at hand; I like to resemble a vestal virgin.

Marta, partly undressed and without her corset, lies dejectedly smoking a cigarette on a rose-colored couch, not looking in my direction.

She absent-mindedly strokes a cat, which lies close to her and purrs loudly, pretending to be pleased but cross in fact because she wants to sleep, and Marta prevents her.

"I shall be so bored when you leave us, Janka," she says. "There will be a sad void all over the place."

"Then come with me to Warsaw."

"Somebody must remain to keep house at Kłosów; besides, Grandfather cannot be left alone. I shall not be free for another year yet, when Janusz has finished his course in agronomy."

"Do you know, Marta, you remind me of a heroine in an old-fashioned novel, and I don't care for variety. You are too goody-goody. Such a pity as it is to waste a year of one's youth. You may quite well leave everything to the steward's care. Remember, you will soon be twenty-five, and life never goes back."

"But I am glad—how glad!—that it does not."

"That's a pose, or a mere high-flown mood. You love life in spite of all."

Turning towards her, I meet her earnest gaze—calm, and yet, oh! how mournful!

"I hate life, Janka!" she replies.

Silence follows. The cat leaps from off the couch, stretches herself, and makes for the fireplace with leisurely velvet tread. She rubs herself against me, lies down in the full glare of the hearth, and instantly falls asleep.

"Once," Marta continues, "I saw them kill a black sheep, as I had told them to do. A clean-shaven old farm laborer first tied its legs, and then sharpened his knife on a whetstone for a long time. Finally, he turned its beautiful tapering head on one side and deliberately, skillfully, drew the knife backward and forwards across its throat. And the poor animal did not so much as shudder: never did it once bleat or show the least sign of reluctance. I wanted to run away, or cover my eyes, or at least turn from the sight: but I forced myself to undergo that internal agony, to atone for the quiet death of that meek, harmless beast. I asked the laborer afterward whether he was not sorry for killing it. He answered me: 'Why should I be? It was my lady's order. I would cut a man's throat for her if she told me to.'

"Once my threshing-machine killed a man. Corn had been stolen, and I had to watch the men by myself, the steward being away at the time. They had stolen it because I had more than they. I remember the man leaning forward incautiously—a horrible cry—a dull grinding sound—and a sudden silence. The machine had stopped; out of it, they took only a bleeding mass. I made the dead man's widow a life pension and saw to the bringing up of the children. And because of that, they call me benefactress and angel!

"Or again. A woman of seventeen died in childbirth. Three days and three nights she lay howling in the farm servants' quarters, howling like a wounded beast, so that I could hear her even in my own room. Well, she died at last; but the boy survived. He is now three years old, he laughs in the sunshine, cuts earthworms to pieces as a pastime, and tears off Maybugs' legs.

"Kosa, a peasant here, had a son who was dying slowly of consumption. The priest was sent for and brought him the last sacraments. Outside the hut, he had to bargain with Kosa about the burial fees.

"Once, in our pond, the loathsome swollen corpse of a newborn child came floating to the surface. What harm had it ever done? Possibly it was put to death because its life of a day or two had made it the instrument of some wrong done!

"Janka, life is unbearable!"

"Listen," I say, lowering my gaze. "I—I don't know how to start; that is, I wanted to let you know that I might be leaving you for only a short while. In a few weeks, I might return."

"I wish you would," she replies. "Janusz is in a pitiful state."

Another pause follows. I contemplate how distant I am from such a desire, and I feel something rising in my throat. Suddenly, I decide to speak now.

"Marta," I say, "tell me why you rejected Imszański." She gives a start, staring at me with eyes like a frightened deer's.

"Don't be afraid," I reassure her. "You mustn't think I will impose compassion on you; I am merely calmly and objectively interested. Tell me: could you possibly not be in love with such an amazingly handsome man?"

She is silent for a while, debating with herself; and then:

"Yes, I was in love with him," she replies, in a calm, low voice.

"Well, and have you sacrificed your happiness for that abstract theory of yours?"

Another pause.

"Not exactly. The fact is, I simply couldn't bear to think I had not been his only love."

There she stops, but I sense she is only waiting for me to question her further; this is the moment when she must lay bare to me what she has hitherto, with her usual secretiveness, concealed from every eye. Yet I refrain from questions.

Again, she speaks, slowly and as one looking back on memories that are still fresh: "We often spent the winter evenings together. His soul was the dearest thing to me on earth, but I loved him even more because his eyes were so mournful and his lips so fine.

"He may have been too outspoken: he wanted me to know all about him before I committed to him. I wish I had known nothing; there is bliss only where there is ignorance. For there have been some moments of forgetfulness, and these have given me an inkling of what my happiness would have been—how immense, how incredible—

had I been his only love in the past, as I am (it yet may be) his only love in the present.

"It was on a most beautiful winter night, silvery in the moonbeams, that I saw it pass before me, that long procession of women, fair as the flowers of spring: 'a connoisseur of women' is what they call him. A whole garden of red flowers sprang up in the snowy wilderness, shining afar like a great pool of gore. I closed my eyes with the torture of the sight.

"If it is true that love consists of happiness and delight, then all this delight ought to have been mine: and Life took it from me—not to give it to others but to throw it away (ah! the crime of it!) to fritter it away among a multitude of delights that might have been. For indeed, what would have made my bliss was a wrong inflicted upon others, in the form of compulsion and shame, the torment of humiliation, the infringement of their right to live, hurling them into an abyss of misery and abandonment, and closing the gates against their return to a happier state: all these deeds of wrongdoing were acts that might have given me bliss!

"Now, it came that in one of those moments of oblivion, when I felt I was happy, I told him I would marry him.

"Then he gathered me in his arms—oh, with what a movement, admirable in its tenderness—and pressed me gently to his heart, that he might kiss my lips.

"And then came the most astonishing instant in all my life. I had, to put it simply, a vision. Upon his lips, I saw blood—clotted, dried blood—the ashes as it were of thousands and thousands of kisses. It was neither loathing nor hatred that I felt; only an exceeding horror for what is as much against Nature as was any elaborate excruciating torture of Medieval times—as a crime committed in secret and hidden under flowers to conceal its every trace. And from beneath those flowers—a sea of them—I seemed to hear the groans as it were of those slain at some banquet of Elagabalus:[8] or rather I heard laughter, artificial, forced, metallic laughter—the laughter which 'women of that sort' always utter, it being the paid merriment to which they are bound: such a laugh as breaks off suddenly, abruptly, as though startled at its own sound. And I saw my white lilies plunged in that sea of tainted blood!

"So, I rejected him, as I would have rejected a foe. And here," she concluded suddenly, in a falsetto of spasmodic laughter, "here my little idyll comes to an end."

"But do you love the man still?"

"I do."

From the farmyard echoes the crowing of a cock—like a key grating in a rusty lock, it disturbs our ears. Dawn is breaking.

I have a fondness for the man; or perhaps it's more accurate to say that I appreciate his surroundings, which are inseparably linked in thought with him. I find appeal in those rooms of austere aspect, with their lofty ceilings and shelves, nearly as high, filled with books—all in meticulous order and bound in black. The grand table at the center, illuminated by bright lamps and strewn with periodicals in various languages, is to my liking. Those substantial, comfortable, leather-covered armchairs surrounding it, and Obojański, who in this setting is a handsome man with greying hair and dark, youthful eyes, also earn my favor.

Obojański, once my professor, has been highly beneficial in my studies. However, the benefits I've gained from him are mainly negative, arising from the critical aspect of his teaching. In our mutual relations, he still enjoys assuming the role of a master.

Usually, I visit him late in the evening, dressed in black, adopting the style of "la dame voilée."[9] If he is engrossed in work, I sit with him, delving into some intriguing book. However, our conversations mostly revolve around serious matters.

Obojański, an old bachelor, typically harbors reservations about women. "The concept of emancipation, while not entirely unreasonable in principle, has been misconstrued and distorted by women themselves. They seek not only economic equality but also the same freedom in behavior as enjoyed by men. What a chaotic world it would be if they achieved that! Regarding the admission of women to higher studies, it's utterly unnecessary: a woman's brain lacks the logical precision required for such pursuits."

"In that case," I respond, "a census of the sexes might not be desirable. It's doubtful whether not only all males but also all learned men possess the capability for accurate logical reasoning."

"Of course, exceptions can be found everywhere," he gravely replies, maintaining his distinctive directness of mental association.

In his eyes, I am one of those exceptions among women. He is never scandalized by my late visits—perhaps only because they are made to him. He holds great respect for my intellectual capacity, believing it to be his influence. I am, for him, the one woman capable of rational discourse.

For my part, I don't consider myself clever merely for drawing logical conclusions from premises. Cleverness, as I see it, involves understanding all things without wonder, setting aside preconceived ideas and doctrines, and abandoning accepted forms of thinking. It's about stepping outside oneself, viewing both oneself and everything else objectively.

Seated in one of the high-backed armchairs, I initiate a conversation on some intricate subject, subtly steering it toward Rosławski.

"Do you know London?" I inquire.

"Oh, yes; I visited there a long time ago, just after completing my university studies."

"I believe Rosławski spent about six months there."

"Yes, and he's still there."

My composure has just been tested, and I am content. The news I've heard doesn't make my lips quiver or cloud my dark-golden eyes with the slightest mist. Still, I take care not to feign indifference or particular good humor.

Obojański, despite his flaws, is no mean judge of human nature.

"Indeed! I was informed he had already returned to Warsaw."

"No. I expect him around the middle of this month. He's a nice fellow, isn't he? The three of us got along very well together."

"I hope you don't mean that the two of us don't get along well," I reply, smiling amicably.

He shows me a postcard he received from Rosławski: water, some shipping, and an unattractive building ashore with innumerable windows. I see his handwriting for the first time: slanted, not very legible; nothing extraordinary. I resist the urge to press it to my lips—an act of highly unjustifiable sentimentality.

Despite my strong desire to return home and, like a child, have a solitary "good cry," I linger there for some time. Obojański offers me several books, mostly related to zoology. I, of course, attempt to excuse myself as best as I can. Finally, he admonishes me about squandering my talents and claims that my mind, "if deprived of intellectual nourishment, will wither away."

"But, Professor," I argue, not without a touch of pride, "I am not naturally suited to be a woman of scientific attainments."

"Ah, but have a little faith in yourself; you should. Truly, science is your exclusive vocation, but you must work; you need to work a good deal. With your abilities..."

I leave, taking the books with me. My room is dim, dreary, and lonely. I am profoundly disappointed.

I have done a foolish thing today.

A girl named Nierwiska works in the same office as me. I find her particularly appealing as she is the most beautiful. Both her appearance and attire consistently reflect a Japanese style that gives her a somewhat delicate and graceful appearance, as if weighed down by her own hair. After returning from the holidays, I noticed a significant change in her, and she seemed exceptionally despondent.

Today, contrary to my usual routine, I left the office with her, discovering that we shared the same route home for a considerable distance. Our conversation initially revolved around trivial matters. Nierwiska responded briefly, in hushed tones, occasionally casting somewhat suspicious glances in my direction. Women possess intuition, and she, less refined than Marta, is averse to purely objective curiosity. I sense that any overly direct questions will prompt her to close her lips, withdraw into herself, and become as unresponsive as a mimosa leaf. This makes me doubly cautious. Our conversation eventually drifts toward the general plight of women who work for a living.

"Those compelled to work for their livelihood," she says in a melodic tone, "tend to fall into a chronic state of melancholy, even when there is no real and tangible cause for it."

"You are right. There are people who cannot comprehend how one can feel sad as long as no harm is befalling them. But for us, life itself is a burden; it harms us."

"Because of the work we have to do."

"Don't you like your work?"

"On the contrary. I would like it, but..."

"Well, but what?"

"In general, I can work with a pretty good will, but right now, I am so weary and upset."

As we stand in front of the house where Nierwiska lives, I draw her into the doorway and ask her in a whisper, "You are in love, aren't you?" She gives a start and shies away from me. I soothe her by stroking her hand gently.

"Things aren't going smoothly, huh? Tell me."

She hangs her head and replies in an earnest, childlike tone, "No, they're not."

"He doesn't love you?"

"Maybe a little. But I must tell you, for me, self-respect comes first. I cannot, even if I have to break it all off, I refuse to made a fool of for anything."

I look at her attentively, somewhat surprised. Until now, I hadn't known her to have this kind of character.

"As for me," I suddenly confess, "if the man who ruined my life and left without even a smile or a kind word of farewell were to beckon me today, I would follow him like a lamb!"

Then, in the rough, comradely manner of work acquaintances, I bid her goodbye with a handshake and walk swiftly away from her door, feeling depressed and uncomfortable—humiliated, to put it simply.

Now, I am in an extremely foul mood. She has proven to be more clear-headed than I am. Through a few common remarks, she elicited a confession from me that I would never have made, not even to Marta herself! It's partly a pose, that remarkable self-respect of hers. Nevertheless, she is sacrificing her love for it.

Strange creatures, these women! Consider Marta: purity! She was raving about it. Nothing should stand in the way if one loves; hence, I probably cannot find love anywhere.

I often call on Obojański now, with a faint hope that I might encounter him there. Each visit becomes a fresh disappointment. This "hope deferred" is pushing me beyond my limits, and the bitterness of my suffering intensifies my longing for him—more impatiently and affectionately. Truly, I am beginning to believe that I love the man.

I no longer care for songs, dances, or flowers. I dream of an unusual life, a cold and secluded life—him and me together—no, a life devoid of kisses. I cannot explain why, but I somehow feel I couldn't bring myself to kiss that hard, firmly set mouth. Nothing ties me to him—nothing but the dominance of his sharp, icy gaze. Yet, I live with the conviction that he is destined to be mine, and no one else shall be my husband.

I visited Obojański today, intending to return to him a monograph (left unread) about a certain insect species. From the anteroom, I overheard a man's voice. My heart leaped with joy, mixed with trepidation, only to be immediately subdued.

As I discovered, it was the voice of Śmiłowicz, a former pupil of Obojański—a somewhat odd-looking man who amuses people not with his wit but with his peculiar, comical expressions.

"I must admit," he says, turning to me, "that at first glance, I found you detestable; you had all the outward appearance of a fine lady. It was only when the Professor explained that you were an accountant and worked for your living that my hatred turned into sympathy for you."

His hearty laugh instills in me an artificial gaiety that almost causes me pain. "I cannot doubt the sincerity of your compliment, even though it was delivered in such a negative manner. It's certainly a novelty. But I have no desire for my appearance to symbolize the dreary life of a working woman."

Obojański, somewhat irritated, remarks, "Alas! Even the cleverest of her sex can't escape this little bit of vanity!"

I glance at him, elegantly reclining in his easy-chair, dressed in a fine suit of black cloth, his trousers neatly creased, a well-tied cravat, and his silvery beard impeccably trimmed. I smile silently. I won't tell him what crosses my mind; he would immediately protest that his clothing is unpretentious—neither dirty nor untidy, but nothing more. All these semi-conscious little insincerities are distasteful to me; there's something unmanly about them.

"Vanity is nothing but an aesthetic feeling in its maturity. Undoubtedly, it contains an element of coquetry, but the latter has its source in the reproductive instinct," I say seriously, speaking quickly to conceal my feelings. I add, "A woman's clothing reveals her individuality and degree of artistic culture."

"Fashion is nothing but the expression of variations in human preferences. Just like in literature, art, and history," I explain.

Śmiłowicz chimes in, "But these variations should be free, not enforced."

"There's no help for that. We encounter individuals with happy thoughts and crowds that imitate them. No one orders them to imitate; they do so willingly, driven by the force of other people's opinions, because they neither think nor act for themselves. Besides, is following fashion necessarily a spirit of imitation? It's often something infectious in the air we breathe. Short sleeves succeed long ones, sleeves puffed at the wrists follow those puffed at the shoulders, just as Idealism succeeds Realism, and Mysticism prevails where Positivism once did."

"Tut, tut, tut," says the Professor, "there's a difference between literature and dress."

"Of course. General trends should allow particular tendencies to come into play, and that's where individuality is manifested. That's why I can't stand male attire with its never-changing stiffness and lifelessness of form."

"Do you not see that this fixed standard is the great leveler of classes, annihilating inequalities in social standing? Attired as I am, there is no difference between me and a shoemaker in his Sunday suit," argues Obojański.

Once again, the insincerity, the cheap semi-conscious coquetry of these words, is disagreeable to me. No one looking at him could help seeing that a shoemaker, clad in those very garments, would be otherwise attired than him. And Obojański is perfectly well aware of that.

"That is precisely what's wrong with men's clothing. It excludes the manifestation of what truly exists, and by removing the outward show of an evil, it helps us forget its presence. I do not think that's right," I respond.

"Yes," Śmiłowicz adds with his amusing grin, "the outcome for you, Professor, would be that people, mistaking you for a shoemaker, might assume you to be an honest man earning his bread solely through hard work."

The notes of Grieg's "Der Frühling" come to mind, strongly recalling the evenings spent with Marta. I was happier then; every present joy is magnified when seen through the lens of the past. I now view Kłosów as a lost paradise to which I will never return.

Something grievous awaits me here. And, in the meantime, he does not come—he does not come!

"There are times when I doubt whether I am doing well to awaken your mind so early, raising doubts about all the beliefs you were accustomed to. I fear you may find such views an intolerable burden on your mind and get lost in the maze of my skeptical musings."

With these words, Obojański concludes a lengthy lecture challenging the existence of God and asserting that the soul is merely a function of the body. I smile at his concerns, assuring him that I am in no danger of doubting fundamental truths.

"I now see that I consider you a friend and talk to you about everything. I forget that you are a woman—and as yet all but a little girl."

The electric bell rings, its ring seemingly unremarkable to me.

"Who has come so late?" I ask, trembling.

"Rosławski, most likely. He arrived yesterday and wrote that he would be here, but I was no longer expecting him."

I hear the servant's steps in the anteroom, and the door opens. Obojański leaves the room, and I recognize that voice—his voice! He explains the cause of his delay.

"Do you have anyone with you?" he asks, seemingly averse to encountering strangers.

"No, no; only Śmiłowicz and Miss Dernowicz, whom you know. Come along."

This time, my self-control abandons me, and I feel my face flush. My initial impulse to rise and welcome him is halted by my lack of strength.

I remain silent, head down to conceal my emotions. Śmiłowicz says something to me, but I can't make it out.

In comes Rosławski; I bow without meeting his gaze, scarcely raising my head at all. I fear I might do something unexpected. A wild, unaccountable terror overtakes me, akin to the feeling just before fainting. I clench my teeth, anticipating.

After a while, my nervousness subsides, and I find myself asking him about his voyage, England, and the sea. The calm indifference of my own voice surprises me.

The first coherent thought strikes me—I am a beautiful woman, I must be. Rosławski talks to Obojański; they must be left alone for a while. I rise from my armchair and approach Śmiłowicz, who stands silently by, looking at a new book on a shelf. Cool, majestic, head held high, and bright eyes shining serenely in the gaslight, I walk by Rosławski. I see myself from an external perspective, clad in a clinging black dress with a great soft, intricately designed autumn hat; graceful silhouette, slow movements, picturesque in their indolence, a result of an abundance of latent vital force subdued by will.

For the first time, I cast my eyes upon him, meeting that cold, critical gaze of his. No one but myself has ever been able to look at me in such a way. I stand by Śmiłowicz, stooping down elegantly to read the title of the book he is perusing. All the while, I know the other's cold gaze is fixed on me.

"You have changed considerably during the vacation, Miss Dernowicz," Rosławski says to me in an undertone audible in the quiet room.

"Have I?" I reply with a smile, lifting my head.

"Yes, you seem taller now, more like a 'grown-up.' Last year, there was still a hint of the schoolgirl in your appearance."

I protest playfully and attempt to engage with Śmiłowicz. However, instead of focusing on him, I find myself lost in thought.

In my perception, Rosławski is less a man and more a mechanical force, a nature imbued with hostility and hatred; a dangerous and mesmeric influence. This tall, well-dressed, well-informed gentleman in glasses doesn't strike me as a living being but rather as an abstract idea. At times, it's hard to believe he possesses any personal existence at all.

I have the impression that I'm standing on a railway track amidst a whirlwind of frozen snow. Above the howling wind, I hear the thunder of an approaching train. Yet, I remain fixed in place, eyes locked onto the cold, unfeeling glare of the oncoming engine's lamps. It's akin to a dreadful nightmare, where I'm powerless, hostile, and yet filled with self-loathing.

Tea is served, and the conversation takes a general turn. Rosławski introduces a freshly imported British iciness and rigidity into the usual atmosphere at Obojański's. We all sense invisible etiquette binding us, creating subtle and unbreakable cobwebs. Laughter is subdued, and everything feels stifled and grey.

"So then," he says, never taking his eyes off me, "you can observe and analyze everything in life with a severe and minute scrutiny?"

"Yes, I can. The predominance of thinking over emotional faculties characterizes my brain."

"Don't you consider this a disadvantage? Such constant vigilance must rob you of directness in feeling."

"To some extent, yes. But this lack of directness is compensated by the pleasure derived from observation and analysis. I attain a broader range, perceiving and discriminating subtle shades that others might overlook."

A smile appears on Rosławski's lips, and I feel my soul freezing within me.

Now, summer has faded away, the flame-red flower of Life fallen, withered by suffering and desire. The infinite plains of ice stretch around me again. The sun is extinguished in the black sky, and the greenish Northern Lights rise on the horizon. My ice-cold dreams, once dead, come back to life. And behold, my victorious Soul, trampling my flowers beneath her feet, strides into the snowy Infinite, proudly celebrating her sorry triumph, singing a lofty and sublime hymn to Death.

Oh, how terrible it is when the Soul is victorious! How terrible!

The weather shifts abruptly; it's nearly as warm as summer, and the leaves seem to have turned yellow from the heat.

I walk home from the office, feeling alone and forsaken.

I have a vision, almost like a dream, of the boundless fields, picturesque ridges, dark forests, and fragrant meadows of Kłosów. I envision the park, with its neatly-trimmed shrubberies and tall trees forming a canopy overhead, their bare trunks and leafy tops tinged with yellow or red in the sunny glare. I also see the large pond, almost a lake, bleak and desolate under a moonless, starless night—the night when I broke free from the enchanting spell of Life, destroying my own happiness with my own hands.

Before my eyes, people stroll along the avenues strewn with dry, dead leaves. The slightest breath of air dislodges these tatters and strips, once a regal purple mantle, but men go on, mercilessly trampling down the rustling leaves.

Now, I'm in a peculiar mood—a kind of Pantheistic state. My Ego multiplies, evolving into countless gods and permeating the entire world, where there is no room for anything except Me. A profound amazement seizes me when I think about how these crowds of people can tread upon my golden autumnal leaves or glance at me just because I have a noticeable face and a hat. *À la diable m'emporte*![10] Can I believe that they live? There is no life but mine alone.

No, they have no life.

And there, an immense way off, on the farther shore of the Ocean of Infinity, he stands, he, the only foe worthy of me: and he waits for me to go onward to meet him!

And I—I stand in fear. For a week, I have not been to Obojański's, where he goes nearly every night.

When the thought comes to me of the splendid sorrel mount I had and of Janusz whose lips were so sweet, I feel like bursting into tears. But I won't go back there unless... Oh, if only I could keep from going back!

I have an irresistible inclination to seek for types among people. I do not like things accidental, either without logical connection or without connection with the special nature of a given mind. If it were up to me, I would, like a scientist working in his laboratory, remove from every character whatever is unnecessary and unessential, to avoid complicating and obscuring its reactions with others. For example, I should like to make Obojański a sage of ancient Greece and eliminate everything from him that disagreed with this type. Śmiłowicz should be a narrow-minded Socialist; as it is, he is too clever for his type, and needlessly cleverer than Obojański. Rosławski is almost perfect. I would only desire—and this, too, for purely personal motives—that he might look upon marriage from a less ideal standpoint.

What my own type is, I do not know. Very likely I have none, and this has troubled my mind for many a year. I am unable to find anything general in myself or to define my own nature in one word and make an abstraction of it. For that, I am far too complex.

My father was a bricklayer, and yet there is nothing vulgar in my face, postures, or movements. I sweep my floor and clean my own shoes; yet, my hands are as soft as velvet. During my entire childhood, I either went barefoot or wore cheap, clumsy boots; yet my feet are white and bear no mark that I ever went barefoot. My work for the greater part of the day—adding up innumerable columns of figures—is such that could numb most brains, and yet I am quite capable of thinking keenly. Though I neither write poetry, sing, nor paint, I have a thoroughly artistic mind. My way of living borders on the destitute; yet I have all the epicurean instincts of those who live at another's expense. After all, I am (as I am perfectly aware) nothing extraordinary, and yet, to be the little that I am, I have not undergone one twinge of conscience; in all that is Me, there is not one atom of harm done to anyone, and not a single tear from any living being.

A postcard from Marta, featuring a "Decadent" figure of a woman, all covered over with microscopic handwriting.

"Grandfather is dangerously ill. I haven't slept a wink for a week and am almost light-headed. Nervous energy alone has sustained me until now. I cannot answer for tomorrow. I continually feel as if my brain were swelling and would fly to pieces. I am tormented by the horrible uselessness of undeserved pain. I don't want to think about what the end of all this will be. I only know that something within me is giving way. Never has my spirit been so broken down. I am now paying the score of the Past, and with extortionate interest besides. The autumn of life has come upon me, taking me unawares, without any reminiscence of a springtime that was never mine. Every night, all night long, I sit by poor Grandfather's bed, going over my interminable litany of sorrow and shedding my heart's blood drop by drop. —M."

And not a single word about Janusz! As I am heading home from the office today, I encounter Śmiłowicz, carrying a big parcel of books under his arm. Despite his ridiculous smile, the man impresses me; the life he leads strictly adheres to the doctrines he professes. Obojański tells me he is a very capable teacher of Natural Science, but he loses all his lessons because he cannot reconcile his advanced opinions with what the school superintendents require. For some time now, he has had nothing, or nearly nothing, to eat; he spends his mornings in the University Library and his evenings at Obojański's.

As we pass by the "Philharmonia" building, he informs me that he has never been inside it.

"Do you object to going there?"

"Most certainly. I am against music, fine costumes, everything that represents satisfaction and amusement. To me, all that only suggests extortion, wrongdoing, and injustice because only a few can afford to go there, and that's at the expense of others."

"But you forget that wrongdoing and injustice are by no means essentials of the Beautiful, of Art, and of artistic delight, though at the present time they happen to exist in connection with these. Your theory seems to make far too much of what actually is. Try to deliver yourself from the fetters of the Temporal; look upon the present day as being yourself outside of it and soaring above it: do you see what I mean? I also resent whatever is unjust, but I can separate the Beautiful therefrom and love it, both in Art and in life."

"Well, you may be right, but I cannot take up such an objective point of view. In me, indignation overbears any gentler artistic sentiment. Yet more: I think it is not now the time to enjoy Art or to plunge into the deep and subtle analyses of Aestheticism. What we want at the present time is Action."

"But, for myself, I quiet my conscience with the fact, which I know to be true, that I am living now just as I should live in that future when, as Ferri says, all are from the very outset to have equal opportunities for their development."[11]

Śmiłowicz is pleased.

"Ah, then you understand. I was afraid you had been surprised at my friendship for Obojański, seeing the way I am accustomed to talking. But, you know, if scientific work were properly compensated, Obojański's monographs would bring him in enough money to live as sumptuously as he is doing now. So, he arrives at the very same result, though by different roads. Yet that, unfortunately, is equivocating with principles."

Oh, I should not object, so far as I am concerned, to any such "equivocating"! As things stand, I am working too much: I might work less and do something better. All my talent is quite thrown away on those everlasting accounts.

My dream is now how to make more money. And this renders me somewhat uneasy; perhaps it is on account of financial circumstances that I am now considering the possibility of marriage with Janusz, in case Rosławski....

This I should not like. Not because it would show my character in an ignoble light. That's nonsense. No, but it would mark how little I care for the creature I could take on such terms.

I am one of those whose sin is greater than the sin of Eve and Adam: I have eaten of the fruit of the knowledge that there is neither good nor evil.

Certainly, for I have persevered until the very end. Everyone possesses something they can claim as their own. Sufferers amplify in their minds the power of suffering; those who have relinquished everything elevate their strength of will to a god-like status. But I am left with nothing, absolutely nothing. I lack sufficient beauty to love that beauty within myself. Wisdom is wisdom only from a particular standpoint: if lost, its very concept ceases to exist. I possess too much intellect to be crafty and mysterious, so I don't strike anyone as uncommon. I exhibit all the shortcomings of a perfect sage; I believe in nothing and am indifferent to all things. However, I am not encyclopedic like sages, nor do I love knowledge, nor do I have any. At the same time, I don't, like a typical Decadent, revel in my doubts and indifference. On the contrary, I play the role of one who is cheerful, well-favored, happy, and entirely content with being what I am. This isn't because I deliberately try to keep my secret to myself, but because merriment is less wearisome to me than the apathy of doubt. And I'm not even sure if what I'm saying here is true.

Rosławski? Well, let's say I am drawn by the interest of an experiment.

I am turning a trivial affair into a serious and important matter simply because of my affinity for some pathos in life.

Why, Janusz himself can be "distinguished" on certain occasions.

Madame (he writes),

May I venture to remind you that the period chosen by you, within which to give me a definite answer, will have come to an end on Monday next?

I beg to remain, Madame,

Most respectfully yours,

—Janusz.

Yes, the time has come. I shall go to Obojański's to-night.

Here I have arrived, with fevered lips and an ice-cold heart, only to discover that Rosławski left just a quarter of an hour ago, having to dine with some friends this evening. I can still smell in the air the brand of cigars that he smokes. My eyebrows and lids are twitching as if agitated by some witch's spell.

Yet I feel not the least disappointment at not finding him here; rather, a sense of relief, that I can put the affair off a little longer.

Obojański tells me what a favorite of Rosławski I am and goes so far as to hint—in jest—that he is in love with me. This very evening he was asking why I have not paid a visit to my old Professor for such a length of time. This, for a man of his sort, must mean a great deal.

In the main, however, Obojański is in a pessimistic and quarrelsome mood this evening. He blames me for too readily embracing new trends of thought, which does me great harm. There is no contemporary poet equal to Homer; therefore, I ought to be somewhat more deeply read in the works of the old classics, which reflect such a healthy feeling of harmony between body and mind.

"You are," he says, "every day less mindful of the admirable maxim, '*Mens sana in corpore sano.*'"[12]

"Why, no; I decidedly uphold proper care of the body, to make it hardy and healthy, and able to resist the wear and tear of our now over-subtle and over-sensitive minds."

"Yes, but nowadays our very minds are diseased."

"Well, then, let my motto be: 'In a sound body, a diseased mind!'"

Or whatever people may choose to call diseased.

Scholars and thinkers, though they surely must have made some studies in logic, yet reason thus by analogy: Disease of the body is any departure from its normal state; consequently, any mind other than average is considered diseased. But if they start from the premise that the mind and body are identical, then why reason at all on the matter?

Now I would burst into song, to run about in the open country, flooded with the white low sunbeams, and to utter cries of joy.

Why? Because the old Professor has said: "He is in love with you!" And because I believe he has spoken the truth.

Yes, and I shall continue to believe it until sundown, and I am still dreaming of a joyful triumph. I had one before, but it was far from joyful.

Tomorrow evening, I shall go to see Obojański once more, and I shall tremble with great fear.

I am sure my answer to Janusz will be delayed. Tonight, Śmiłowicz and Rosławski accompanied me home together. I cannot say whether I shall get any opportunity for a private talk with him. Perhaps it is better so: but then, Janusz is waiting for his answer down in Kłosów.

Rosławski is the one man in the world before whose gaze my eyes must droop. That alone can throw me off my balance, rob me of my customary untroubled assurance; it is the only force able to master mine.

As we approach the end of our conversation, the topic shifts to love and marriage.

Śmiłowicz contemplates marriage from an economic perspective, deeming it a necessary evil in our current societal conditions. However, he shares an instance of mutual acquaintance who recently married and appears perfectly content with his choice.

Obojański cautiously interjects, "Ah, yes, in the initial months, such a thing is not entirely impossible." Rosławski wears a cold smile, expressing his favor for marriage, a natural inclination for a man who has left behind his wilder days and desires a lawful form of love. Interestingly, even the most unconventional men I've known theoretically endorse monogamy. Imszański, for instance, always assured Marta that, were it not for the unpredictability of women and other unfavorable circumstances, he would find his greatest happiness with one woman alone.

Obojański, on this matter, remains a skeptic, and it's the only subject he can humorously engage with. Rosławski, addressing me with a subtle tone of flippancy, a common stance of his towards women, asks, "And you, do you intend to marry for love?" A sudden tremor of fear seizes me, but I compose myself and respond with a calm smile, "Your question makes me feel as if under examination. Admit it; you're more interested in my response at this moment than in my actual intentions."

There's an ironic gleam in his eyes, and he asserts, "You may take my word for it that I am not."

"In that case, I'll tell you as much as I know. If I marry for love, it may not last very long. On the contrary, if I choose a partner with discernment, based on a conscious conviction of compatibility, then I will remain faithful to my husband for a lifetime."

Rosławski probes further, "And which of these alternatives do you prefer?"

I reply, "The second," adding truthfully, "for there are certain feelings where I object to changes."

"Really? But you would have the same result even if you married for love."

I confess, "I am afraid I cannot believe in the eternal duration of mere feeling. Love in marriage, over time, transforms into a kind of mutual habit, a sense of solidarity, and occasionally, even a union of minds. In such cases, divorce might be advisable."

"And in a marriage of reason?" he inquires.

I explain, "The question is correctly stated from the outset. Suitability of characters and individualities are considered, preventing any potential future disagreements."

"But it's possible to maintain love by incessantly watching over it, occasionally wearing a mask, and keeping private certain emotions and states of mind that might prejudice one party in the eyes of the other." As I listen, the memory of Janusz returns, unaware of any of this.

"I doubt whether so much trouble is very profitable," I respond.

"The game is hardly worth the candle," Rosławski continues. "And yet some prefer present bliss even if they know it will be taken away tomorrow. They often choose to renounce it entirely." Though spoken calmly, there's an ominous undercurrent in his tone.

I assert, "Well, then let all such take care to marry with judgment."

"Nevertheless, giving love and receiving only intellectuality in return is not a good bargain, I fear." Now, I understand, and I almost feel hatred for the man. I may throw myself under the wheels of a locomotive, but I'll never claim it's out of love for it!

"Reasonable people should remember that 'the heart is no servant,' and beyond intellectual and conscious resolve, we can find nothing on which we can safely count." I say this as lightheartedly and smilingly as possible, feeling the dismay of a horrible misgiving—almost a certainty—clutching at my heart.

Finally, I am alone with Rosławski and Obojański. I remain in my corner, overwhelmed with dread of the impending decisive moment. That tall, red-haired gentleman in glasses—simply detestable!

Rosławski begins playing Wagner—stiffly, correctly, like an automaton. His playing grates on my nerves; each note taps on my heartstrings. Obojański is enchanted, moving about the room on tiptoe, making the floor creak. He fetches music for Rosławski, glancing at me and whispering almost aloud, "How very beautiful!" He brings me a volume of a German encyclopedia, opening it at the article "Wagner," expecting me to read.

I am so upset that I nearly break down. Resting my head on the back of the sofa, I look up at the ceiling to swallow down my tears as they well up. And I begin to weave fantasies.

In a wondrous ancient forest, knights clad in armor ride on white steeds. Majestic oaks, with black trunks and dark-blue foliage, stand tall amid mosses resembling malachite, while ferns spread their sea-green lace. Fairies dance joyously among the trees, casting pearls of laughter. Far away, on a dark, enchanted lake, a swan floats in reverie. A strange, clear, chilly splendor illuminates the twilight.

Suddenly, a red thunderbolt falls, and the forest and lake vanish into the depths of the earth. Yet, thunderstorms only occur on sultry summer days. No, all of this was but a dream.

Now, before me, stretches the infinite wilderness of my plains of ice, frozen beneath cold, glassy skies. A feeling of dread overwhelms me; I cannot breathe as I witness those endless ice expanses under a canopy of green and frosty light—the kingdom of my soul.

In the distance, at the sky-line where the Aurora Borealis beams without warmth, stands a colossal statue, hewn from basalt. Unaffected by the vast wilderness, the chilly Northern Lights, or the stars, it stands tranquil and undismayed. This is Rosławski.

I march towards him through the deep, drifting snow, and at his feet, I kneel. I implore him to shield me from the boundless wilderness, protect me from the icy air of death, allowing me to dwell in the land of my soul without perishing. "For today, I am exceedingly weak; today, I stand in fear of the plains of ice."

He replies, "In the snows around me, you must first lay out a garden as of the tropics, and yourself must blossom into a fiery red and purple rose."

I question, "My lord, without the light of the sun, how is any rose to bloom?"

Another thunderclap resounds. He is gone, and I am alone amid my plains of ice, still alive but bound with fetters of ice. The silvery wings of my soul glitter under the heaven's canopy, and a snake lies on my bosom, coiled around my neck, sucking the warm blood.

We bid good-night to Obojański and step out into the street together. "I have something to tell you, or rather, one question to ask," are my first words.

"I am at your service."

As I speak, the sense of dread dissipates, replaced by immense quietude. "I must lay down one condition: I will accept no answer other than a simple Yes or No. I do not wish, and this is crucial to me, to hear any comments. Do you agree?"

"Most willingly," he replies with a smile. "I will certainly adhere to the condition."

"You must know that since I met you, I've considered you the only man who could make me happy. Some time ago, another man, deserving of my sympathy and trust, proposed to me. Believing that the knowledge of being greatly loved might substitute for happiness, I took a month to consider. My decision depends on your answer. I foresee what it might be, but I am eager for absolute certainty, lest I reproach myself for missing my chance at happiness."

A silence follows.

"May I ask you to phrase your question more definitively?"

"Are you willing to marry me or not?"

Another silence.

"No. And yet, supposing that..."

"Remember my condition."

No more words are exchanged. In front of my lodgings, we bid each other a calm and friendly farewell. The next morning, on my way to the office, I drop a scented envelope into a post-box. It's addressed to Janusz. However, the decision it contains is not to marry him. I am now a bond-slave to my soul, unable to leave these plains of ice that no longer belong to me.

I am done with suffering. Throughout these long days and nights, I haven't shed a tear. I don't suffer now; the delirium from agony has surpassed those limits where no difference is felt between joy and misery, where there is no night of woe contrasting with day.

In the still autumn twilight, I am confined to my dark and lonely room. Pacing the soft carpet with noiseless steps, I fear the very movements I make. Trembling with cold or emptiness of heart, I lean against my doorway, wrapped in the folds of my shaggy portiere. In the darkness, I open my swooning lips to utter a soundless cry and stare into the fluttering dark with a tired and quiet gaze.

I don't suffer; I exist in a world where the night of woe is no longer a contrast with the day, where a tranquil dusk prevails without sun and stars. There is no Ego of mine. I am beyond existence and nothingness, in a world where the immemorial conflict between dream and vigil dies. There, Wrong, robed in queenly purple, is not shadowed by Vengeance in her pallid green attire. Stony Hatred no longer embraces the weeping god of love, and the marble statue of Pride no longer pays homage to the grim specter: Fear. There are no more wretched victories or the portentous delights of self-worship and the Power of Self.

No, there is no more Ego of mine. I am in a world that even the unlimited fields of Infinity cannot reach, for it was always beyond all limits. I am in a world where Duration neither flows nor stands still, where Solitude is not, though there are no spirits to commune with. There is no solitude because there is no Me.

Do I suffer? No. I am in a world where I have no being. I could well die if I chose, but my body, well-favored as it is, would prefer not to part from my bright, though mournful soul. Therefore, I am willing to live.

But there is nothing for which I can care any longer. I dwell in a world my soul will never behold because when Death comes, my soul's existence will be over. Yet not because there is nothingness there. To believe in nothingness, one must have an intense power of faith. I cannot accept the creed of nothingness. In this world, where I am now, neither Being nor non-Being exists; there is neither Ego nor non-Ego, and the soul has never laid her icy hand upon the body. I am in a world where there is no soul of mine.

My soul will end its being at the instant of Death, not because that world is a world of nothingness, but because there is no indestructibility of substance. I might die if I chose, but death means nothing to me. To solve the riddle of life, I don't require death. I know all now. I know that, in that other world, knowledge and ignorance are not incompatible, and there is no desire to know. Therefore, I will never solve the riddle of life because I have solved it now.

I know what no one else knows: to read the riddle, I don't need to know all things. There is no Me! I am indeed in a world that contradicts ours, but with a contradiction where negation and assertion are the same. In one thing, however, I do believe—the only thing that is.

And that thing is: *No!* Such a *No* doesn't contradict *Yes*, but encapsulates the true essence of *No*, when considered alongside *Yes*.

It's the same *No* that Rosławski expressed to me.

If I experience no suffering, it's because I am part of a world where joy and sorrow are indistinguishable.

II
THE GARDEN OF RED FLOWERS

Imszański displayed patience and persistence, refusing to accept rejection as final. Eventually, he timed his proposal well, catching Marta in a favorable mood. She relented, abandoned her objections, and willingly married him.

For almost a year following their marriage, I lost sight of them as they traveled across Europe. Marta, who had never been abroad before, sent me postcards every few days. Despite being immersed in intense bliss, she continually contemplated the thought of death, a not uncommon phenomenon in such situations.

Upon their return, Marta brought with her a few-months-old son. She appeared very pale, resembling a shadow, yet even more beautiful than before. Although thinner, she seemed taller, wearing her dark plaited hair like a crown around her tiny head. At around thirty years old, Marta, despite the age difference, looked well-matched with Imszański, who was considerably older.

They rented a flat in Warsaw and insisted on me sharing it with them. However, I continued to spend most of my days in the office, just as I had before.

Life brought nothing new for me; my memories were mostly colorless or grey. I found myself disappointed, belonging to the class that "gives great promise" throughout their lives. Nevertheless, I couldn't overcome my "*tristesse de vivre*,"[13] but I began to view it with more indifferent serenity.

Initially, you look straight ahead, but at a certain point, you start looking behind you. This point isn't necessarily when happiness eludes you or when a devastating blow wakes you from a sweet illusion. It's a moment that may pass in laughter or tears, or even be slept through. You don't know when it comes, but you do know when it has passed.

For me, it has passed, and now I look behind me, though I'd prefer not to look anywhere at all. I look back and think that perhaps all the fuss was not worth it. Yet, in any case, I've gained some wisdom, and wisdom is eternal. Enough of it remains for me to smile in my solitude, along with some remaining pride—the pride of knowing who I am.

Returning from a concert, I joined my friend Wiążewski to meet our usual company at the Lipka. I take some interest in the reeking atmosphere of a high-class restaurant, filled with gilded youth, old financiers, beautiful actresses, and demi-mondaines. The salon is large, lit with wide-branched chandeliers, thick with tobacco smoke, and alive with the sparkle of lights and the notes of a merry orchestra. The ceiling is painted in an antique style, and the background is speckled with bright stains—white linen on tables, candles with glass "lampions" of various tints, forming spots of many colors. A seething tumult of twinkling lights and ringing cups and glasses surrounds us.

This is a life apart, not the daily round of appearances but life immediate, naked, real. Here, despite everything, it is possible to be merry and carefree. There are no unsightly garments, no clumsy motions; no children, that most objectionable element in life; no "respectable" women recognized by their ugliness, lack of style and charm, tediousness, stupidity, and perpetual depression when they think. It's an illustration of the "Law of Selection" in marriage, where qualities like virtue and fidelity hold more weight than beauty and health, leading beautiful women with lively temperaments to join the ranks of the fallen.

For my part, if I weren't concerned about being accused of having anti-social tendencies, I would boldly declare, from my gloomy philosophical standpoint, that I regard the "frail sisterhood" as an institution without intolerance. There's something about it that harks back to bygone times, something existing but left unspoken. There are human beings, scorned as a class regardless of their personal qualities, with whom no other class is permitted to come in contact, under the threat of defilement—akin to pariahs. These beings are traded for precious metals through secret contracts, bought like slaves in ancient times. Their existence is kept a secret, not for practical reasons, but for the sheer sake of the secret itself, although everyone knows about them. In our hyper-civilized era, bereft of poetry due to excessive culture, this is a most astonishing state of affairs.

Most men present here have wives, actual or intended, but these women are not allowed to enter; they would be far too out of place. Undoubtedly, their wives, after putting the children to bed, have had some disputes with the servant over daily expenses, put on a poorly cut nightgown, said their prayers, and laid down to sleep under a red woolen coverlet, all the while thinking, "He always returns so late after these meetings!" Or perhaps, in a fit of fury, they bite their nails, contemplating another angry scene with their husbands—a scene predestined to be as ineffective as those before. Alternatively, in agonized resignation, they may lean over the baby's cradle, murmuring mournfully with naïve pathos, "For your sake, my child!" As for the engaged girls, they have likely gone to sleep under the watchful eyes of their guardians, lulled by sweet fantasies like, "Most men have affairs before they marry; he, and he alone, surely has none." And so forth.

Foolish they may be, but they are fortunate not to be allowed to enter here.

Ah, once upon a time, in the days of my childhood marvels, how bitterly did I weep over all these things!

"Stefan, what time is it?" I asked Wiążewski.

"It will soon be midnight. Our friends don't seem to be coming. Are you in a hurry to get home?"

"I never am. I have a latch-key, so I don't wake anybody when I come in. But aren't you sometimes engaged in the evenings?"

He shook his head, his teeth shining in a friendly smile.

"You know perfectly well that there's no rendezvous I would not cancel to spend an evening with you. To me, friendship is a far rarer and more precious gift than love."

"I don't agree with you at all. I have enough of the cold consideration granted to me by the world."

Stefan smiled again.

"There's no help for it, Janka," he said. "Men of our times are too weak to love an all-around woman; the very thought of one gives them an unpleasant shock. The era for women as extremely complex as you are has passed; now, women are preferred who display very distinct and special characteristics, especially primitive natures or those corrupted by civilization. Types of spirituality or sensuality, women with well-balanced minds or those nervous to hysteria, and those in whom warmth of heart or a distinguished bearing prevails. That's why the monogamic instinct is dying out completely; in a few years' time, it will be no more."

Wiążewski was on the warpath, the topic being a favorite of his.

"How can a man be true to his wife if he takes her 'for better, for worse, till death do they part,' only to, let's say, kiss a mole she has on her neck just under her left ear? Monogamy requires exceedingly strong, rich, abundant natures."

"Then our near future would witness a return to the hetaerism[14] of primeval times?"

"No doubt, for both the primitive instincts of the senses and their ultra-refined activity have the same result."

A strikingly original-looking woman, accompanied by an elderly, clean-shaven man (probably an actor), passed by our table. She had the appearance of an actress too.

"Fine woman," I remarked.

He turned his eyes away from her.

"She's not my type," he replied. "Far too cultured for my taste."

Then he returned to the subject.

"Hetaerism, indeed. Absolutely. However, if it were up to me, I'd propose a small modification. You see, one of the most delightful types of womanhood is the wifely archetype: a woman who is faithful, trustworthy, completely devoted to you. It would be beneficial for such a type not to fade away entirely. Still, I would prefer her to exist only as a distinctive category, offering a contrast to others and serving as a sanctuary when weary of them."

I observed the attractive Frenchwoman; suddenly, a delighted expression illuminated her striking and serene face. I instinctively followed her gaze and, not without a bit of surprised amazement, noticed Imszański. He was just entering from the doorway, gracefully moving through the salon, distributing bows and smiles like a beautiful woman scattering flowers. His wonderfully sweet and dreamy eyes were searching for someone in the room.

A sudden spark lit them up as they met the gaze of the handsome Frenchwoman.

Imszański, on his way to them, happened to spot me and Wiążewski in my company. Without a hint of surprise or embarrassment, he changed his expression and greeted us with polite cordiality. Despite having passed our table, he returned, shook hands, and asked if he could join us.

The Frenchwoman at the neighboring table was putting on her gloves, while the actor settled the bill. I would have willingly suggested to Imszański to proceed to his acquaintances, who were evidently expecting him. However, I refrained, not wanting to burden him with gratitude for keeping this matter concealed from Marta, which might later prove irksome. Stefan, too, understood.

"We are here," he mentioned, "waiting for Madame Wildenhoff, Owiński with his intended, and Czołhański. It is rather late now; I doubt whether they are going to turn up."

Imszański turned aside to say something to a waiter, noting with satisfaction that the actors had left the salon. He then expressed hope that we would not consider him an intruder, even though he had joined us in such a manner.

Czołhański, a journalist, arrived at about one o'clock, accompanied by Owiński and his fiancée, Miss Gina Wartosławska, whom I had seen several times before at Imszański's. Her real name is Regina, but she goes by Gina. In the movements of her lithe, elastic figure, there is a sort of snakelike suppleness, indicative of a nervous nature burning with a passion almost painfully suppressed. She is like a tame panther. Her eyes, long and narrow, partly concealed beneath thin lids, wander here and there about the floor with a drooping, apathetic look. Her lips are broad, flattened as if kissed many times, moist and crimson as if they were bleeding. And yet, there is something priestess-like about her.

She came in, pulling black gloves off her slender hands, greeted us with an unsmiling face, and immediately called out to a passing waiter:

"A glass of water!"

She drank the whole glass in one go, then sat down at some distance from the table, with her head bent forward and her hands clasped over her knees. Owiński took a seat close beside her.

"Czołhański," he informed us, "has just finished his critique of tonight's play's leading actress. We had to wait for him in the editor's waiting room."

"Ugh," complained the critic, "this commissioned work at breakneck speed is quite unpleasant! A piece like that deserves careful consideration until a definite judgment can be formed. As it is, we're forced to salvage the situation with a lot of pompous generalities."

Finally, Madame Wildenhoff arrived with her husband. At the unexpected sight of Imszański in our company, a deep blush covered her face. She took a seat next to Gina and burst into a fit of giggles, shading her eyes with beautiful hands adorned with numerous rings. This was quite unusual and disconcerting. Imszański blushed slightly; a warm haze, so faint that it could barely be seen, clouded his eyes, and his long lashes drooped over them.

Wildenhoff, an unpleasant and methodical man, whose humor inclined toward sarcastic silence, suggested that we move to a private room. She protested.

"Oh, no! I dearly love noise, music, and an uproar all around me. We better stay here, hadn't we?"

Wildenhoff smiled at his wife and was soon engrossed in studying the menu.

She resumed laughing without any apparent cause: a disconcerting chuckle, with something like a sob now and then.

I glanced at the two couples, feeling a twinge of envy. "There is love between them."

Oh, but all that was so very, very long ago!

I wish Stefan would fall in love with me. But he is always pursuing some theory or another. At times, he is as whimsical as a boarding school girl. I truly believe his friendship for me is absolutely disinterested. He, for his part, claims that a beautiful woman, as such, means nothing to him. The type he loves is uncultured, shallow-brained animality.

He is still too youthful. Men's preference for more spiritualized, cultured, and quick-witted women is only a reaction: it indicates a decline in vital forces and foretells the onset of old age.

Throughout our journey home, he, rather lost in thought, expounds with artificial animation.

"With you, Janka, I could well live alone in a wilderness, even if you were twice as beautiful as you are—and never remember that I was in the presence of a being of the other sex. And, indeed, this is the most natural thing in the world: if such a thought ever entered my brain, I should feel humiliated that a woman was mentally my equal."

"But is it with perfect disinterestedness that you have chosen a pretty young woman for your best friend?"

"Why should I not do so? That gives me the advantage of a double pleasure: not only can I enjoy your conversation, but I can enjoy your appearance as well."

"You might just as easily take a handsome man for your friend."

"Yes, but then beauty in a woman generally accompanies intelligence; whereas good-looking men are, as a rule, rather foolish. Moreover, however objectively I strive to judge things, I must confess that a woman's body is more handsome than a man's."

"And what of her mind?"

"Why, she has none: I mean there is no such thing as a feminine mind. Though, look you, it is not unlikely that women also have minds. There is nothing sexual about the brain, either way."

"Yet you have always said I had the mind of a man."

"I was wrong; as a friend, you are neither male nor female. You are something that I set in a class apart, and I want you to do the same by me."

At our doorstep, I bid farewell to the entire group. Imszański expresses the desire to continue with "the ladies" a little further, but he's back immediately. I can guess why.

The Imszańskis host "At Home" events on Sundays. From three until dinner-time, the door is essentially open to all. These gatherings are formal, tedious, and rather pretentious affairs. Moreover, very few people attend, as Imszański lacks acquaintances with whom he maintains cordial relationships.

But I find these Sundays enjoyable; they soothe my nerves like warm baths. With the people who attend, I need not attempt to maintain any appearance of truthfulness. On the contrary, I say very far-fetched and most fantastic things—things that I know are unlikely to interest anyone present.

However, this is where Imszański truly excels. Never are his movements more elegant, his smiles more cordial, or his glances more winning. No one can distribute the small change of social niceties better than he, with his looks and superficial judgments on literature and art. When addressing a compliment to a woman, none can more subtly wrap his intentions in a mist of allusions.

Both husband and wife present themselves admirably. He, with the perfect culture of his ancient and noble descent, is simply enchanting. Marta is a contrast to him, representing something newer but deeper: the culture given by unassuageable sorrow, the concentrated reverie seen in the sad looks of those dark-blue eyes, albeit a kind smile always flutters on her parched red lips.

Occasionally, the Wildenhoffs also attend on Sundays, creating a most interesting effect. Rumors circulate that Madame has an affair with Imszański. Marta is aware of this, and everyone knows that Marta knows, yet she feigns ignorance, fully aware that no one believes her. Thus, an immense heap of lies is being piled up, creating a curious situation that is not unpleasing to me.

Lombroso[15] would have classified Madame Wildenhoff as belonging to the class of courtesans "by right of birth." Her snowy flesh, golden hair, brows looming above azure eyes, rosy cheeks, and scarlet mouth—all of this fairy-like coloring gives an appearance of complete artificiality. Her wonderful shape and inborn talent for coquetry make one regret that such gifts have been lost on such an unsuitable field of action. I have no doubt that the need for money is but a secondary motive for those who join the "frail sisterhood." If it were the main inducement, what would lead men to lead lives so similar to the lives of demi-mondaines?

I enjoy observing Imszański playing the part of the host with her. Nothing in the whole world seems capable of throwing him off balance. He greets her just as he would any other visitor, with a set "So-pleased-to-meet-you" sort of smile. He dedicates as much of his time to her as he does to any other woman present. Conversing with her, he partly flirts and partly freezes her with the haughty consciousness of his preeminence as a drawing-room "lion." He doesn't attempt to conceal his liking for her but shows just as much as is appropriate for any young and handsome woman. It would be a breach of the laws of hospitality if he didn't offer a few discreet compliments to each of these women and convey a look of warm admiration, beaming from those ever-half-curtained almond eyes.

Jerzy is sometimes summoned from the nursery, and in he comes—a little fair-haired boy in black velvet, sporting a superb collar of yellowish lace. The ladies engage him in French conversation, praising his accent.

Today, the following conversation unfolded:

"*Qui aimes-tu davantage, Georges,—papa ou maman?*"[16] was the question posed by Madame Wildenhoff, her hand adorned in a white glove of Danish leather, as she stroked the boy's curls with a sweet smile.

"*C'est papa,*" was Jerzy's reply.

"*Et pourquoi donc?*"

"*Parce que maman ne rit jamais.*"[17]

Everyone hastily began to extol the accomplishments of Jerzy, who is not yet four! They did so to conceal a certain discomfort felt: the *enfant terrible* had unconsciously touched on a matter that everyone knew but no one talked about.

Madame Wildenhoff, who undoubtedly anticipated the boy's answer and perhaps elicited it purposely, was the only person to underline its meaning. She let her long eyelashes droop over her rosy cheeks, pretending to be shocked at the unseemly associations it had, through her, brought up.

Marta laughed in merry contradiction of what Jerzy had just said. Then, kissing his fair brow, she instructed him to make a nice bow to the company and return to the nursery with the maid.

Society is burdensome to Marta now. We used to go together to the theater or a concert, but presently, she has no desire to go. I mostly spend my evenings with her, engaged in endless conversations. She either recounts something to me, or she "gives words to sorrow." I listen.

She is currently distressed that her husband Witold has hardly been at home for nearly a fortnight. Some days, we even dine without him.

"It is surely so," she said yesterday. "He enjoys his manhood to the full: everything is his. There, he has 'Bohemian' society, reveling, fast people, singing, champagne, flowers, and forgetfulness; here, he finds the pure and quiet light of the domestic fireside, the delights of fatherhood, the love of a faithful wife. When he is tired of one sort of pleasure, why then he tries the other. And *we*; we are all crippled, helpless things, all!"

Silence for a moment.

"There he gets his amusement at the expense of those poor weaklings, whose souls have been wrenched away from them, who have lost the feeling of their human dignity, the consciousness of their right to live, even the very sense of pleasure; who groan under that most unjust burden, their own self-contempt; who feel the continual oppression of a guilt that does not exist, and for whom the first wrinkle is a death sentence.

"But on his domestic hearth, there beams another fire, and beams on another kind of weakling; a strange creature, now no longer able to descend into Life's hurly-burly; for whom certain deeds, for many a century regarded with scorn, have through long heredity of ancient feelings become really loathsome.

"Our duty is to amuse *them*, the lords of life and death, with the effects of contrast; that *they* may have the assurance of having experienced the whole gamut of emotions, that they may enjoy their manhood to the full."

When Witold came home today from the club (around noon), Marta received him in a beautiful white *peignoir*, trimmed with Angora fur, and asked him whether he had had breakfast yet. He thanked her graciously, kissed her hand and brow, and desired to see Jerzy.

Marta changed color. She is not so jealous, even of women, as she is of her beautiful little boy, perhaps because he is with her constantly. The nursemaid brought Jerzy, who at once jumped onto his father's knee, and began talking at the top of his voice about several things which had happened to interest him since the day before.

Imszański was enchanted with the little one and kissed his rosy face. For men like him, there is something incomparably sublime and public-spirited in the fact of being a father; this they hold to be the only thing that compensates and atones for the life they lead. Marta shrank away, standing at a distance, fury in her heart and a smile on her face, watching the father caress his boy.

"See here," she whispered to me, "this—this is my calling, the mission of my life. All the pain I've endured, the fury of my never-ending and futile rebellion, my disappointed existence—it's all been for this moment. For them to sit here like this, completely forgetting me, and for all the wrongs inflicted on me by the father to come alive again in his son!"

And Witold, after showering affection on Jerzy, retired to bed. Only in the evening did he awaken, looking fresh and hearty, ready to dine with us. He kissed Marta's hand, shared lively stories circulating in town, and then headed back to the club.

In matters of love, Wiążewski is just as capricious and insatiable as Imszański, but their "spheres of influence" differ. Wiążewski favors seamstresses, shop assistants, and the like, while Imszański is particularly drawn to coquette (even his affair with Madame Wildenhoff is an example). Despite their courteous demeanor, neither has a great fondness for the other. Imszański holds it against my friend that he's too democratic, while Wiążewski sees Imszański as a fool.

The latter explains his aversion to *demi-mondaines* in this way:

"I have a great liking for misdeeds, but not when committed by professional criminals."

The art of playing with his victims has been perfected by him to the highest degree. To achieve this, he employs what naturalists term "mimicry." With rather commonplace features, he easily catches a girl off guard, disguising himself as a business man, a messenger, or a waiter, expressing himself fluently in the slang of those classes, which he has mastered perfectly.

He is a true expert in connecting with the minds of such people, navigating a labyrinth of ideas unknown to us with admirable ease.

In principle, he advocates for constant change, but lately, he's made an exception, claiming to have found the right kind, or nearly so. He has been keeping company with a girl whom he, due to her exceptional qualities, has set apart from the common herd. I once saw her at his lodgings and was impressed by her beauty.

He read a letter from her today, and when I asked for it as a "document," he readily consented. It reads as follows:

Dear Stefan,

I have something to tell you; Roman, the prospective husband of Genka, came to the shop yesterday evening and started questioning me about her. "I have no idea where Genka is," I replied, "What business of mine is that?" He insisted, saying, "Genka is in Krucza with that mechanic and he's keeping her. I hear he's in love with her, but I'll get him for it. Unfortunately, I can't remember the street and the number where he lives. Can you tell me? I know his name is Stefan." I told him, "Don't bother an honest fellow. He has nothing to do with girls, let alone such hussies as Genka." He asked where you lived, and I said Krucza number 129, fourth floor, and Stefan Tworkowski is your name. He thanked me and left. He mentioned he'd ask the porter in Wspólna, and I warned him not to poke his nose in, or he'd get his head punched, just like when he flung dirt at me before. So, if he comes, tell him that and give the beast a talking to.

And something else, my dear darling. As I write this, I love you to distraction. I am regularly off my head thinking about you, and I have your photo in front of me, kissing it night and day. Oh God, how I love you more than my life, more than my faith. I can't fathom what sin I've committed be punished like this. Dearest, you are so cold, and your coldness will bring me to my grave in no time. I don't know, but it seems you told Elizabeth I slept on Hoża Street, and she makes a mockery of me. I don't care a fig because I am daft for your love. No one will cure me, and no one can. It's too late. I loved you when I first saw you, and I will until my life ends, as long as I don't put an end to it. And who will make me do that but you, Stefan, my dearest pet?

I end this scrawl of mine, throwing away my pen, crying my eyes out, and dying of hunger for that blessed Sunday.

Your unhappy or rather love-sick,

—HELA.

Fully aware that I am committing an indiscretion, I allow Marta to delve into her past. I even take the initiative to question her, laying out the long and gloomy vista of her wounded love. I listen in the manner she prefers, calmly and without any display of compassion. Compassion, after all, is as absent for her as it would be for a fish that must reside in cold waters or a bat recoiling from sunlight. Marta revels in suffering, and perhaps it is this very inclination that compels her to endure it. In fact, she exhibits a kind of Sybaritic sensitivity to pain.

"But there was a time when he loved you, right?" I inquire.

"Oh, even now Witold insists that he has loved no one but me!"

"Well, well. At what point did this—the current phase—begin? There must have been some period when he remained faithful to you."

"Yes, for a few months. Right at the beginning. Although I was never truly happy. First, in the six weeks leading up to our wedding, I was constantly tormented by mystic fears, to the point of nearly losing my sanity. You know I don't subscribe to those clichéd moral maxims, yet I always felt that something malevolent was afoot, and a day of reckoning was imminent. And besides, how unbearable it was to think that now I *had* to marry him, despite my strong aversion to the act, and that I had more at stake on my side than he did."

"And afterward, by the seaside?"

"Oh, that was enchanting! I almost felt happy. But it lasted such a short time! Shortly after our arrival, I fell ill, becoming unwieldy, weak, and plain. And then, if you can believe it, surrounded by all those wonders of nature and art I was constantly yearning for Kłosów, my own home!"

After a few minutes of silence, she continued:

"I saw a drawing by Brenner. It haunted my thoughts; a woman who had passed away after surgery, stretched on a table, lifeless and rigid. There was a man grieving over her, his hair resembling Witold's. And another picture, portraying the tragedy of motherhood: a young mother has just breathed her last; on her bosom sits a naked child, a repulsive idiot, gazing out at life with wide-open, bewildered, lackluster eyes. I can't help but imagine that Jerzy resembles that child."

With a sudden and brisk motion, she summoned the manservant.

"Find out from the nurse why the child isn't in bed yet. I hear him making noise. Tell her to put him to bed or take him farther away from this room."

Once the servant had left, I asked her, "Why did you speak so angrily to him?"

"Truly, I cannot recognize myself anymore; my nerves are horribly unstrung," and she sank into somber contemplation.

"Tell me more," I urged, trying to draw her out.

"More? Well, I wasn't so badly off then. We reveled in the blue sky, the murmuring green sea, and our almost absolute solitude. Witold was always by my side, tender and kind—disguising with his exquisite courtesy the disgust I must have made him feel. Why, for myself, I often felt pity and aversion; I, who had never before been anything but graceful all my life.

"Then things went downhill. Listen, but it's too much for me right now."

"Then don't talk about it, Marta."

"Ah! What does it matter after all? If I could forget... but I can't.

"A few weeks before Jerzy's birth, Witold spent the night away from home for the first time. I stayed up all night, looking out through the window over the sea. Ah, that night!

"The servants had gone to bed long before. There was a great storm, with boisterous gusts of wind, and I listened to the never-ceasing roar of the waves. You know how much I fantasize. I immediately imagined Witold must have been sailing in a boat to the farther shore of the bay, and gone down to the bottom of the sea. I was horribly alarmed for his sake, and for a time, not an inkling of the truth flashed upon my mind. The horror of my fantasy overcame me so strongly that I quite forgot all about his past. For I believed with unbounded faith in his immense love for me and would have dismissed, as a ridiculous notion, the idea of his possibly being unfaithful. I was out of my mind with terror. I counted the hours that went by, in agonized expectation, surrounded by the dark cloudy night, and hearing the terrific howling and rolling of the winds and waves. Oh, that night!

"In the morning, he came in.

"With the demeanor of a youthful page, he doffed his hat to the ground in a courtly bow and stood motionless in my presence, humble, clasping his hands. Then, in a sweet, soft voice somewhat broken by emotion, he said, in an accent of dismay:

"'Oh! My lady, I am afraid, greatly afraid!'

"I did not rush to welcome him, nor did I cry out aloud; I felt too weak for any display of joy. But at that first instant, in the sole knowledge that he was living, an infinite intensity of quiet, fathomless, and endless bliss flooded my heart. I was minded to exclaim, like Mary Magdalene at the Sepulcher, 'My dear Rabbi!'

"And then the sun rose!

"He had never appeared so admirable to me, adopting the stance of a medieval page with the playful humility of his radiant smile; he had never been so beloved by me, so exceedingly dear. No, I had never experienced such joy in all my life, as in this fleeting moment of solace!

"And yet, they say women possess intuitive minds!

"I felt as if I were ensnared and suspended in an aerial cobweb stretching over an abyss of waters. There, I gazed upon the golden splendor of the morning landscape, now that the tempest had subsided—surveying the blue and shimmering tranquility. Below me, under the bridge of hanging gossamer, flowed the somber sea of dread and death; before me rose the sea of life, painted in hues of crimson and blood-red. Yet, I beheld nothing there, except the dawn and the sunshine."

Here she paused, closed her eyes, and, resting her head on the arm of her easy chair, remained immersed in the contemplation of that past scenery, all azure and gold. I allowed her to rest for a while, then, prompting her:

"Well, and what happened next?" I inquired.

She furrowed her brows slightly.

"Then, oh! then! It was a trivial question, for I worried about nothing now that I had him again. But I asked him what he had been doing all night.

"'Oh, but I am afraid, in such fear of you,' he said, smiling, kneeling before me, and clasping his hand—just so! You're familiar with the gesture; it almost embodies child-like humility.

"'Oh, what?'

"'I want you to promise you will not be angry with me.'

"I was suddenly struck with a sharp misgiving.

"'No, do not tell me, Witold,' I whispered.

"But he couldn't conceal anything from me. All he offered in excuse was that I should forgive everything due to his great love; that no woman could ever seize the place I held in his heart. He hadn't truly been unfaithful, as his genuine and sole love had always been with me; I was the only woman his soul loved, not his senses. It is always the same: reach out your hands for life, and Death will come to you!"

"And what did you do?"

"In the initial moments, I didn't comprehend it all. He repeatedly professed his love for me a hundred times more than ever before; I was the only woman, so pure, so ideal, and I couldn't figure out what he meant. But when his lips touched my hands, they grew as cold as ice.

"He was frightened and tried to appease me; said he would never do it again; it wasn't properly his fault; he had been overtaken with wine. Besides, she—she was indeed most beautiful.

"At the mere recollection, I saw his eyes flash brightly. Oh, he is a connoisseur of women!

"And then, at last, I comprehended it all; and I thought (believe me, with the utmost sincerity): 'Why, rather than this, has he not been drowned in the depths of the sea?'

"A mist veiled my eyes; I rubbed them to see clearly. Then, a sudden pain seized my heart, making me writhe in agony. I fainted; when I came to, fits of hysteria overtook me. In short, I enacted all the scenes that a typical 'injured wife' is wont to perform.

"When Jerzy was born, I was dangerously ill. Witold didn't admit he had wronged me, nor did he come near me at all. Later, he justified himself by claiming he could have been of no use and was too sensitive to bear the sight of suffering.

"Finally, when all danger had passed, and Jerzy's joyful clamor filled the house, the same night repeated itself, and he was once again 'a little flushed with wine,' and 'guilty of no offense'; again, I was 'his only love.' And later, the same scene was replayed over and over at shorter intervals. And to this day, it is just the same.

"And now, I am peering into the very depths of my soul. Have you ever seen it? An open coffin, in which there are no worms, no corruption. Only patches of color, continually fading, changing, reviving, and forming lovely stars—just as in a kaleidoscope. And these hues glisten like the scales of a serpent which rolls and coils itself in ecstasy."

A smile passed over her face. Then she gave a long shudder and closed her eyes tightly.

Suddenly, she stood up, joining her hands behind her bare and shapely neck.

"If you knew, Janka," she whispered, "if you only knew how I love him! If you knew how I long for him every moment when he is away! If you knew how fondly, how wildly, how madly I love the exceeding sweetness of his mouth!"

Madame Wildenhoff does not belong to the class of women that Marta was speaking of. I think that, were it not for her intrigue with Imszański, even Marta herself might acknowledge her as a "complete woman." One may, however, be a complete woman, and yet not a complete human being. We are not yet in the habit of distinguishing these two ideas, as we distinguish between "human being" and "man." The part of a human being is one so seldom played by a woman—they have so few opportunities of doing so—that we expect their womanliness to comprise the whole of humanity. Nor do we realize how much we lower woman by such an expectation.

Now, as a woman, Madame Wildenhoff is complete, although her human nature cannot be said to be rich.

Her life, which she told me with the utmost frankness, has not been wanting in color. The daughter of a rich landowner, she was not yet sixteen when she crossed the frontier to elope with a neighbor over forty, with whom she was not even in love! The whole affair came about quite by chance. She was the friend of his daughter, whom (though he was not in favor of religious education for women) he had decided to send to a convent in France. The parents of Lola had asked him, since the two girls had made their studies together from the very beginning, to take their daughter with him as well. This man, having put his own daughter into the care of the nuns, asked Lola whether, instead of poring over books in a convent, she would not like to go with him to Italy. She very readily agreed to what she considered a most natural plan. After a few months had elapsed, she tossed him aside for a very handsome Italian, who later turned out to be a Parisian Jew. After many other such experiences, her parents, as a last resort, took legal measures to find her. This time they placed her in a convent, and there, during three years of penance, her outlook on life took a definite shape.

Her father eventually softened and allowed her to return home, as the family had abandoned country life and settled in the city. Within the year, she entered the bonds of matrimony.

Her initial love interest was Wartosławski, who passed away some time ago; Gina Wartosławska, whom I previously mentioned, is his daughter.

It didn't take long before Madame Wildenhoff strayed from her marital vows. However, her husband, from the vantage point of his silent skepticism, regards her dalliances with a scornful nonchalance. It might even be that he doesn't mind this state of affairs.

A daughter, two years senior to Jerzy, is the sole offspring of this union. Madame Wildenhoff showers her with the utmost care and tender maternal love.

Today, I paid her a visit in place of Marta, who is frequently unwell. She was alone, as Wildenhoff, like all husbands of his ilk, either was absent or had not yet returned.

She attempted to engage me in conversation, as is her custom, largely about herself.

"My external appearance, given all the credit it deserves, is insufficient to explain the extraordinary success I've had with men throughout my life. My only skill—call it an art if you will—lies in influencing men by appealing to their baser instincts. That's the only way to succeed with them, for they are all mere animals—all!"

She offered me some fruit, lifting the vase with a gesture reminiscent of a courtesan from ancient times presenting a goblet of golden wine.

"You see," she continued, "I am an epicure. I want to extract as much as I can from life, and I know how to achieve it. Life would quickly grow dull for me with nothing but champagne, songs, and flowers. So, occasionally, I enjoy the atmosphere of a soirée, for example, with the Imszańskis. As for her, I'm unsure whether she is genuinely purer than the atmosphere of a private supper room; nonetheless, her style of corruption is unique—more Gothic—and the virus is more deftly inoculated. I like to take a break, spend some quiet evenings with my family, teach little Sofia her alphabet, or endure sleepless nights in penance, vigil, and somber contemplations. After that, I might execute a sudden pirouette, Parisian style, and blow a farewell kiss to my husband, Sofia, mamma, grandmamma—and virtue!"

She laughed heartily.

"I'm not anticipating the future of nations. No, I'm determined to extract the maximum happiness for myself under the circumstances I find myself in. You might say I'm a mere product of my environment; well, so be it. But bear in mind: my way of life harms no one. If I am content, so is my husband, and so are my admirers as well."

"And their wives too?" I ventured.

"Well, is it my fault if they are fools? Now, let me tell you. I have never taken a man from a woman he loved. I am not one of those whose sole aim is to conquer difficult hearts."

She added after a pause, "For a very long time (and you must surely know this), Imszański has been completely indifferent to his wife."

Just then the bell chimed in the ante-chamber, giving Madame Wildenhoff a start, who then erupted into laughter. In that peculiar laughter of hers, I discern something intriguing, though I cannot quite fathom what it is.

I rose to bid her farewell.

"Why are you rushing off? It's just Gina. I enjoy seeing two clever, beautiful women together, a rare occurrence, I must say."

Gina entered with her customary aloof greeting, as usual, asking for a glass of water. She then proceeded to peruse various albums scattered about the table. Her flawlessly stylish figure stood out like a sort of anachronism against the backdrop of that ornate middle-class drawing-room. In the light, one could discern her golden eyebrows and lashes, and her wavy hair of a dark auburn hue cascading in a disheveled mass onto her shoulders as she bent forward.

Madame Wildenhoff tried to steer the conversation toward general topics. She began with women's rights and their failure to grasp the true meaning of emancipation. Gina, though not a prolific speaker, belongs, like Madame Wildenhoff, to the category of those emancipated in every sense of the word. In reality, her intended husband is her lover, and she has no intention whatsoever of becoming his wife.

I had noticed for some time that she possessed a spirit of contradiction. In the presence of people with definite convictions, she consistently took the opposite side, perhaps to create a more striking effect through the sharp contrast of tones. This attitude brought to mind certain reminiscences from an ancestral past. I started discussing the gradual extinction of individual monogamistic women, the permeation of eroticism in our democracies, the necessity for a class of courtesans to preserve the type of women interested in more than just love intrigues, and other similarly nonsensical ideas.

Gina only looked at me with a drowsy smile, but Madame Wildenhoff enthusiastically took up the argument. Interestingly, her discourse resembled Marta's, although their natures were vastly different.

"Men are naturally endowed with a sense of equilibrium; as long as they are in their prime, they live, love, and laugh at plain and virtuous women. *Car il faut que jeunesse se passe.*[18] They need what we might call the 'brute-woman,' a woman who laughs, glitters, and shines for a few years until she ages. Then, of course, she retreats from the arena, regretting that 'she ever followed such a path.' Only after men have sown their wild oats does the animalistic instinct die out, and they awaken—as a plebeian, a thinker, a father, or a citizen. Then they reach out for what we may call the 'human woman.' It's the triumph of she who respects herself; her day of victory has come, she is finally 'appreciated,' meaning compensated for her virtue with that famed respect never granted to those of the other class. The intellectuals may complain sometimes that men won't acknowledge them as mental equals, but the foolish ones will be honored with their husbands' friendship and confidence. The good mothers will find their aim and happiness in bringing up children, all the while looking down upon the 'brute-woman' or viewing them with philanthropic compassion."

"Poor things!" Gina exclaimed, "they don't know that the tragic excitement of a single night may perhaps be worth more than an entire existence spent in such torpid apathy as theirs."

Today there is some festival or other. I have not gone to the office, and have been sitting all morning at Marta's bedside, who is not to get up until the afternoon. She is as usual always complaining, her sad eyes gazing into mine.

"Janka, I can't sleep at all anymore. Last night, I tossed and turned until midnight. Like a child, I cried myself to sleep eventually. When I woke up, it was only three o'clock."

She crossed her lace-decked arms behind her head and gazed into space with infinite wistfulness.

Then, in a hushed voice, she continued, "I can't fathom why my past life in Kłosów haunts me so vividly now. I remember how, at times, I used to rise early on a winter morning, when it was still dark, and dress by lamplight, shivering with cold, resisting the urge to return to my warm bed. I would put on a massive fur coat, grab the keys, and go to the farm with a lantern in hand. You know, all of this is present to me now, like a vision. I recall the distant fields lying fallow beneath the snow, stretching to the horizon under the sky where the stars were beginning to fade. I remember the farm buildings, dark spots on the landscape, the forests resembling streaks of violet, the gray fences, and the delicate pattern of leafless garden trees. And now, through the darkness, sounds emerge: the clattering of tin pails and the faint, drowsy calls of the maids to one another. Oh, and I remember well the cold, the robust, fresh, piercing cold, making the teeth chatter. And then, the cozy warmth of the cowsheds, the low, black-raftered ceiling overhead, the outlines of solemn-looking cows and sleepy milkmaids, the bright circles of the lanterns on the floor, and the quirky broken shadows on the beams and girders above. The milk streams rhythmically into the pails, the indolent lowing of the cow, and the jingling sound of the chain that binds the savage bull to the crib. Do you remember the cat, too—our cat? So sharp-witted, following us everywhere like a dog? All of that is so distant, so irretrievably gone! Oh, I tell you, I would give more than my life if I could see one such morning return—just one such bleak, dark, and frosty morning. If only I could now be as I was then!"

She turned her cheek to the pillow and shed tears.

"Marta, your nerves seem to be in a fragile state again. If you'd like, I can accompany you to Kłosów. We can spend Christmas there together, reliving a few idyllic days from the past."

"Oh, no, Janka; those would only be miserable echoes of times long gone. That foolish, insincere woman, Janusz's wife, would just get on my nerves. Besides, the thought of Witold staying here with Madame Wildenhoff, probably relieved that I'm away!"

"But," she added, with a sudden surge of spirits, "you know, I think her triumph will be short-lived. It's true that

Witold was never very attached to her, but now it seems his affections are strongly engaged elsewhere."

"Really?" I asked, intrigued, recalling the Lipka and my unexpected encounter with Imszański there.

"Did he tell you anything?"

"Oh, he's simply ridiculous—so hopelessly frank with me. He never spares me any details and sees it as his duty to conceal nothing from me," she said, laughing bitterly, then immediately returning to a sullen mood.

"Yesterday, before you came home from the office, I asked Witold all about her. She's some star from the Parisian demi-monde[19] who's set on securing a stage role here at any cost. Witold is expected, due to his influence in Warsaw, to secure a position for her. Apparently, her voice is tolerable, and her appearance is marvelous. He described her to me in every detail. It was truly one of the most emotional experiences I've ever had."

She closed her eyes, intensifying the mental image she was forming.

"The woman is tall, seemingly of slender proportions, but only seemingly so. Her bony framework is exceedingly slight and reed-like. So, you see, Janka, upon closer inspection, she's not really thin."

As she spoke, she turned on her pillow, tearing at its satin covering with her nails and attempting to suppress her tears of rage. I couldn't help but feel overwhelmed by my emotions.

"Why on earth does he tell you about such things? He must be a monster."

"There are many things he can never understand—what I told you seems like the merest trifle to him."

She took a spoonful of bromide and continued:

"You must know that he tells me she has large oval-shaped eyes, with extremely long lashes—eyes of an unfathomable black, in striking contrast with her voluptuous mouth; always sorrowful, dreamy, with a far-away look, like the beggar-maid loved by King Cophetua. She also possesses much originality, something like a concubine, combining the primitiveness of a mountain goat with all the cultured grace of a maid of honor at a royal court."

After removing certain exaggerated points, this description was easily recognizable as the fair Frenchwoman I had seen at the Lipka. Now I understood why Imszański had shown himself so courteous toward Czołhański; the latter, being a theatrical critic, could be useful to him.

"She dresses most superbly, with all the magnificence of Babylonian times: golden combs and strings of pearls in her hair; in her ears, rings of the greatest price. Moreover, she is a very miracle of depravity. Witold smiled as he told me so, with an inward look, as though recalling some particular example.

"As he told me so, he smiled; and I too smiled, listening with the blandest interest. He looked at me attentively, kissed my hand, and said:

"'Your nerves are better now, I see. How glad I am! You have no idea. You have at last realized that to feel jealous of a coquette would be unworthy of you.'

"'Why, of course. Yes, yes; I am all right now.' And yet, Janka, I never felt it so deeply; I never saw things with such awful clearness of vision. And alas! I never, never yet loved Witold with such passionate love.

"But, more than him, I love that pain which I feel."

She rose in bed, as if to repel something that was weighing her down; then she sat propped up by her cushions and pillows.

"Do you imagine that in all this I had any idea of revengeful pleasure at Madame Wildenhoff's disappointment, and for that reason made him tell me what he did? Not in the least. I wanted to drink my fill of pain; as in Spain they wave a red flag in bullfights before the bloodshot eyes of the poor brute, to make him yet madder with rage and despair, so I wished to excite myself to the same delirious state.

"I do not wish for anything that can diminish the intensity of my anguish; I hate whatever could mitigate or deaden it. I love to gloat over the raw, bleeding wounds, bare and unbandaged."

At that moment, the nurse tapped at the door, asking whether Jerzy might come in to bid his mother good morning.

"No—no! Shut the door! I will have no one here! Janka, you have not the least idea how I *hate* my son."

Tonight, at the Lipka, this time in a private room. Madame Wildenhoff talked at great length, somewhat along the following lines:

"There exists only one form of perfect love—that seen in brute creation; instinctive, reflexive love where victory is claimed by the strongest and most beautiful; the pure reproductive instinct untouched by cultural or mental analysis. Unfortunately, we, as civilized beings, tend to disdain this kind of love. Our calculations, carried out with quasi-mathematical precision, determine how much love should be accepted and how much rejected to achieve the utmost quintessential delight. Hence, a new type of love has emerged: instinct emancipated from obedience to the laws of nature—love with its primary motive, the preservation of the species, removed. The love I speak of is commonly labeled as bestial, but in reality, it is a special outcome of refinement."

"It surfaces among nations during the peak of their development and acts as a herald for their swift decline," remarked Czołhański with solemn dignity.

"What does it matter? *Après nous le déluge!*"[20]

"And to what category would you assign conjugal love?" asked Owiński. Gina, who had silently arranged her lithe, snake-like figure on a small sofa, looked around with astonishment at her fiancé.

"Oh, we may call it love of a third type," answered Madame Wildenhoff. "It is love sanctioned by law, the union of two souls in friendship, and the birthing of sickly offspring—an abnormal fusion of brutish and human love."

"Do you then, Madame," urged Owiński, "see no merits in marriage?"

"None whatsoever," she replied with a bland smile, "because—and this reason alone would suffice for me—because I detest marriage with all my heart. It has been and remains the aim of my life to dismantle marriage whenever I can succeed in doing so. In the happiest and most moral couples—those where one of the two, the husband or the wife, leads a profligate life and the other remains oblivious—I introduce the dissolving element, enlightenment, and rejoice when I witness the couples parting ways."

Here she leaned toward her husband's chair and said to him in an affectionate and audible whisper:

"But we are a model couple, are we not?"

This time, Imszański accompanied me home. I overheard Czołhański say, on parting with him: "You can rely on me absolutely; I will manage everything."

It has been incredibly cold, and now there is a thaw. During such times, I love to wander through the deserted park avenues.

My nostrils catch the distinctive scent of moist bare earth and the aroma from buds yet invisible; and I contemplate those incomparable and marvelously beautiful things that have never come to fruition.

Against the yellow backdrop of dry, dead grass, a young man appeared in the distance, seemingly finding pleasure in the solitude, strolling along avenues strewn with last year's fallen leaves.

He caught up with me and, passing by, looked sharply into my eyes with a hint of astonishment.

I didn't return his gaze but walked more slowly, allowing myself to lag behind him.

The young man stopped and waited until I caught up; then he passed by me again with a lingering stare.

This maneuver repeated several times. Soon, I felt an inexplicable urge to burst into nervous laughter, which I suppressed as best I could. Regardless, I maintained full control of my eyes, their expression conveying nothing but indifference and disdain. Eventually, I looked him straight in the face, aiming to stare him down; my attitude clearly signaling hostility.

"But why," I kept pondering, "why should I view him—this handsome, slender youth—as my adversary? He surely doesn't intend to harm me in any way; his interest is merely piqued by encountering someone who shares his penchant for solitude, while naturally harboring a friendly disposition toward an attractive woman."

Initially amicable, the young man was stung by the hostility in my gaze. He approached me closely, chuckling in a flippant manner, and said with an ironically sympathetic tone, "I would give anything reasonable to know what heartaches have led you to embark on such a remarkably romantic stroll as this."

I remained silent, furrowing my brows.

"Souls languishing in loneliness," he continued, still sarcastic, "ought to console each other, don't you think?"

A pause ensued as we walked side by side.

"But why furrow those fair eyebrows? Oh, really, you frighten me. Such malevolent eyes! Come, come, I shall do you no harm; why be so cantankerous?"

Infuriated, I turned my back on him and briskly walked away. He made no attempt to follow. Upon reaching the gate, where I was finally safe, I glanced back. He stood where he had been, waving me a graceful farewell with bared head from a distance.

The incident left me mortified and embarrassed. I had acted foolishly, narrow-minded, and ill-tempered, spoiling a situation that might have unfolded into something pleasant or intriguing. Why had I done so?

Was this, once again, a mere formality? The necessity of a formal introduction, cherished by the bourgeoisie, in a drawing-room where two individuals are acquainted by a third? Or was it the recurring dread—now an integral part of our lives—the instinctive fear of things as they are, the eternal need to play the role of a besieged fort, defending itself obstinately to surrender on the best terms possible?

As I exited the park, a speeding carriage passed by. I glimpsed a couple of feathers and a considerable amount of fur. Suddenly, the coachman halted, and Madame Wildenhoff leaped out, heading towards me.

"Ah! How delighted I am to meet you! You won't escape me this time. Please step in; I must transform you into a proper lady."

"Certainly, but what's going on?"

"You'll hear."

We entered the carriage, and Madame Wildenhoff instructed the driver to go slowly.

"Quite a warm day!" she remarked. "Well, you see, I have one obsession, at least that's what my husband calls it."

"And what is that?"

"Oh, what a coincidence to have met you, whom I was just thinking about!"

"Very well, but what do you need me for?"

"Wait a bit; I must start at the beginning.

"Let me tell you that I consider it crucial for the cause of women to meet and understand women of so-called 'loose character.' And, in particular, establish social relations with them. It is indeed an eccentricity on my part, but I enjoy going against the current."

"It may lead to interesting developments," I remarked.

"You are absolutely right. Firstly, all of us need to comprehend our common interests. The social ostracism faced by the entire demi-monde is a genuine civil war waged by women against one another—a weakening of our collective power, not only unopposed by men but also exacerbated by them. They hold 'those dreadful creatures, bereft of a conscience,' accountable for transgressions they themselves commit. Consequently, the jealousy that should rightfully be directed at them, from their mothers and wives, current or prospective, is instead channeled into a hatred for such women. It's undoubtedly a cunning tactic on their part, but we should not be easily deceived; we must close ranks and stand shoulder to shoulder to combat the common adversary."

"But what if those women despise us more than we do them?"

"That's true, but only because they believe we are happier than they are. We must dispel this egregious delusion, make them aware that we feel our grievances as keenly as they feel theirs, recognizing them as our fellow women, sharing in our common humanity. We have allowed such a falsehood to take root by doing nothing.

"We should align ourselves with them, for they are our necessary complement. Not only that, but we should mingle with them without intensifying the differences by trying, as much as possible, to rid our souls of vast realms of womanliness, sacrificing the allure of frivolity and fragility to our own detriment. There must be a thorough fusion; only through such leveling can we achieve the synthesis of womanhood: a new and complete type where the only observable differences are those of individuals, not vocations."

"That all sounds well and good, but where are you taking me?"

"I'm getting to that. I am paying a formal visit to an ex-courtesan, a Madame Wielołęska—formerly Maria *tout court*, as I don't know her family name. And I absolutely want you to accompany me."

"But, is she suitable?"

"Absolutely; trust me. She takes everything in stride and will be delighted to receive you. However, you must behave as if she were Wielołęski's legitimate wife."

"What? They are not married?"

"Absolutely not! The man has a wife and five children somewhere in the countryside. Yet, that woman has such a hold on him that he won't move an inch away from her side. You must see their place. She was once a common demi-mondaine, though well-regarded."

"How did you come to know her?"

"Oh, she's an old acquaintance, introduced by Imszański."

The carriage had halted in front of an ornate gateway, leading to an elegant suburban villa partially obscured by branches and tree trunks and framed by towering fir-trees.

Ascending the broad white steps at the entrance, I felt an inexplicable acceleration of my heartbeat. Perhaps it was the fanciful notion that within those very doors, I might confront the naked, dark, and enigmatic mystery of life!

An elderly, elegantly dressed footman opened the doors, guiding us into a generously proportioned sitting room, conventionally furnished in the style of the Secession movement.

In a matter of minutes, a very tall, slender lady entered—a vision of refined grace, clad in a clinging morning gown reminiscent of a riding-habit. She was accompanied by a little white lamb, moving with a stiff and occasionally amusing slide across the polished floor.

Pani Maria greeted Madame Wildenhoff with a smiling effusion. "I've come to visit you with a friend of mine, Miss Dernowicz, Madame Wielołęska," she announced, introducing me. "I hope you don't mind; I was eager to show her your greenhouse."

"My dear Madame, you're doing me a favor. I feel so bored in this solitude, seeing no one at all. All day long, my husband is in the greenhouse or tinkering with the compost. He hired a new gardener from Haarlem, and getting him outdoors is out of the question. If you're interested, we can visit the greenhouse right away. I tell you, if it weren't for my books and studies, I might be tempted to end it all."

"Why not take a walk sometimes? The weather is splendid right now."

"Oh, no! My husband won't go out, and it wouldn't be proper for a woman to go out alone. You know how judgmental people can be."

"And what are you studying, Madame?" I inquired.

"Pretty much everything possible," she replied, laughing. "I have at least five hours of lessons every day. One of my professors just left; he's giving me a course on ancient literature from India. And for a week, I've been learning to read hieroglyphics. Have you tried them? They're fascinating. One is transported to other lands, other times. I am so curious about everything in the world. But languages are my forte. It's incredibly important to read every writer in the original."

"Pani Maria is a renowned linguist," Madame Wildenhoff interjected.

"Really?"

"Indeed," she said, modestly smiling. "It comes so naturally to me. Currently, I'm proficient in French, English, German, Italian, Spanish, Swedish, Dutch, and Russian. This year, I'm learning Finnish and Japanese. I've also read Homer and Virgil in the original Greek and Latin. Not one hundredth of their marvelous beauty can be conveyed in a translation, and I'm so attuned to the beautiful!"

"Do you know," she interrupted herself, turning towards Madame Wildenhoff, "I've finally convinced my husband that we must take a trip to Algeria. And it has to be in a few weeks; it's too hot there in the summer. Oh, you can't imagine how challenging it is to tear him away from those flowers he loves so much!"

I scrutinized Madame Wielołęska closely. Her face, framed by sparse locks of fair hair, appeared pale. Her small, greyish, and seemingly expressionless eyes, surrounded by a faint pink hue, constantly moved to and fro. She had a petite nose with rounded nostrils and a full, somewhat bloodless mouth, occasionally twitching with a quick motion, akin to a child making a wry face. Despite this, she exuded an undeniable allure. Her talkativeness, a tuneless voice, and a certain nonchalant demeanor corrected the initial impression of pretentiousness, giving way to the effect of a schoolgirl's carefreeness rather than the audacity of a femme fatale.

She bent down to fondle her pet lamb, which had assumed a well-trained posture at her feet. Then, she straightened up, saying, "Perhaps it's time to take a look at the place."

As we proceeded towards the conservatory, we traversed several rooms and galleries adorned with paintings. On the right, we encountered a workroom, brightly lit even though night had yet to descend. Several girls were diligently hunched over embroidery frames.

"These are my little ones," Madame Wielołęska remarked, smiling at them. "Unfortunately, I have no children of my own, so I've taken it upon myself to raise these girls."

"What are they doing here?"

"They are learning embroidery under the guidance of a German instructor. I am particularly keen that my philanthropic endeavors do more good than harm. My husband wisely says, 'It's not hard to give, but to give judiciously.'"

"Well, what do you do with the embroidered work afterward?"

"Oh, you see, I don't fancy lace on my linen—besides, it's not fashionable nowadays—so I have everything covered with embroidery. Linen looks much more beautiful that way. I might, perhaps, show you—yes, I think it's alright here—only women present."

She chuckled, winking significantly, and led us further down the passage. With a swift ballet-like twirl, she lifted her dress above her knees, revealing several tiers of cambric flounces beyond her silk stockings. At no other point in our visit was there anything to remind us of what she had once been.

"I believe," she remarked, turning to me, "you wear a petticoat; I'm not sure you shouldn't give it up. A well-flounced undergarment makes the dress look sufficiently wide; a petticoat altogether erases the outlines of the hips." Passing her hand down my waist, she said, "It's a pity, for you have a splendid shape—hips like a Spanish woman's."

We found Wielołęski standing at the end of the conservatory, carefully observing his gardener at work. He was a tall man, slightly over forty, rather stout, very elegant, and courteous, yet distant and preoccupied. A considerable bald spot graced the top of his head, with long thin wisps combed over it from the left, without any attempt at concealment. He also sported an abundant black beard.

While guiding us through his greenhouse, he remarked, "It's only recently, since I've been living here, that I truly understand Tolstoy. Only through close acquaintance with nature and manual labor do we discover the emptiness of societal life, its forms, prejudices, and the futility of social dissensions and hatred."

I, not as adept at maintaining a detached observer status as Madame Wildenhoff, couldn't resist presenting an objection.

"Nevertheless, your ability to stand aside in social struggles stems from your ownership of property. Property itself falls within the sphere of these struggles, as they make it an object. So, the very land you own pulls you back into these societal classes from which you're fleeing."

Wielołęski, somewhat surprised, offered me a few freshly gathered white Kalia flowers before responding in a calm but decidedly dogmatic tone.

"On this matter, I beg to differ with you. Those who challenge the right of property disregard the realities of life. Immemorial tradition has established the right of property as much as a 'category of thought' as Space or Time."

Maria, who was just behind us, intervened, saying, "Oh, Edmund is already delivering a lecture, I see. My dear, you better come and flirt with Pani Lola, and I'll take Miss Janina with me."

She came and wrapped her arm around my waist, expressing her fondness for me. I responded with an indulgent smile, the appropriate reaction when women compliment women.

Sensing that this approach wouldn't win me over, she shifted the conversation to literature.

"There are certain books," she remarked, "that offer me solace and allow me to escape from reality altogether. That's why I can't stand authors like Zola, for instance, who bring filth into a realm where only poetry should reign supreme."

I ventured another objection.

"Don't you believe that exposing the sores of society is the first step toward healing them?"

"Ugh! Why write about them? We are all too familiar with them! Life itself is replete with sorrow and murk. Perhaps, being young, you haven't had the opportunity to come into contact with them. No, no: why spoil the brief, sweet moments when we can dream?"

She then suggested we take a break on a bamboo seat nestled among exotic plants and shrubs in large green tubs. Once seated, her trained pet lamb came and lay down on the hem of her dress.

"Shouldn't everyone have some sacred book—a Bible or something?" she asked after a short silence. "Alas! There's no one, with even a modicum of philosophical knowledge, who can possibly believe in the existence of God—and all the rest of it.

"But we can, at least, respect the poetry within religion and the sentiments of those who have not lost their faith, right?"

"Certainly," I replied with utmost seriousness.

"Well, the Bible I cannot fall asleep without reading, and the one I read portions of daily instead of saying my prayers is that book of legends by de Voragine. Do you know it?"

"Oh, yes," I concurred, "the Golden Legend."[21]

"Oh, what a world of poetry it holds! What treasures of freshness and simplicity of feeling!"

When we drove back after our half-hour visit to Wielołęski's, I remarked to Madame Wildenhoff, "Well, I say! If they are all of her kind!" I felt rather bored and contemplated the meaning of the well-known aphorism:

Dans la bête assouvie un ange se réveille.[22]

For some time, Imszański has been spending his evenings at home! He either goes out later in the evening or not at all, and Marta's hopes are reviving within her. Still, I don't take this transformation very seriously.

The three of us often sit together; occasionally, Czołhański, Owiński, or Rosuchowski drop by.

Owiński's peculiar trait lies in the perpetual vague, absent look in his eyes, a consequence of his extremely short sight. He can barely see two paces in front of him and identifies people solely by their voices. His facial muscles are in constant motion, and he only smiles with clenched teeth. Despite his lack of attractiveness, I'm not surprised that Gina loves him to distraction.

Witold has chosen me as his confidante lately, perhaps feeling remorse for his recent behavior, albeit belatedly.

Life, in general, appears as a barren waste to him. His theory of love doesn't allow him to view innocent romantic gestures, often termed "bits of love-making," as harmless, despite their lack of connection to genuine love. These acts are considered evils, necessary perhaps, but men have grown accustomed to them over the ages. He believes women, particularly those of higher classes, should guard against these evils. According to him, his relationship with Marta aligns with these ideals, as he aimed to spare her and preserve her lofty ideals and sense of purity.

I couldn't help but smile at this, knowing how little his intentions had been realized.

Now, however, he seems to be growing weary of his current lifestyle—the desolate wilderness of his existence. He perceives women as shallow, mindless, and fatuous. "Their own moral laxity determines every one of their actions."

I can now discern the direction of his thoughts. "Take, for instance, Madame Wildenhoff. She changes 'affections' every month. That's her business. But why does she bring in Philosophy, Sociology, and Emancipation? What she does is as old as the hills, so why bother with her and women like her?"

I had long ago observed that men tend to dislike women who argue. On the contrary, they hold their souls in high esteem. Now, Witold confesses that it is the soul—the soul alone, at any cost—that he desires.

Who knows if he will once again become a faithful husband to Marta?

I detest colorless people, including myself, as I find I am becoming increasingly colorless day by day. I feel disconnected from my own type of character; I am ordinary. I've had my fill of this life; more than enough.

I am craving desperately for someone to tell me—incessantly—that I am good-looking, clever, and original in mind, that I dress nicely and move gracefully. Even though I am currently convinced that none of these things are true, if told so today, I would immediately believe it.

I am in pain. Sometimes, I feel an urgent need to express all my thoughts. At times, wearing a mask becomes unbearably difficult. I long for sympathy.

Today, I was at the Wildenhoffs' and had a conversation with Witold. I can't fathom how it happened, but suddenly I found myself speaking too much—or rather, too directly.

Realizing that the position I had taken was too advanced and exposed, I decided to withdraw.

"But can you comprehend the true tragedy of my life?" I asked. In silent inquiry, he raised his beautiful mournful eyes to mine.

"In everything I've shared with you, there's a measure of untruth, and in all that I've kept silent about, the same untruth prevails. My manner is to speak of my melancholy one day and then expound on my life's philosophy, free from clouds, the next."

"To whom among men do I reveal the truth? Wiążewski? I'm uncertain. Perhaps to no one. As I strip away, one after another, all the personas I wear, there is nothing substantial left of me."

At this moment, Madame Wildenhoff, adorned in a very low-cut black velvet gown, approached us.

"Why hasn't Marta been here today?" she inquired. "We haven't seen her in quite a while."

"She intended to come, but she is continually plagued by migraines."

"Ah, yes, those migraines," she sympathized. "They are exceptionally challenging to overcome!"

Presently, she asked if I would come and look at a beautiful screen, a birthday gift for her, painted by Gina. Imszański remained where he was.

I asked Madame Wildenhoff why Owiński was absent.

"Really, I cannot say," was her response. "He was supposed to come, but it's rather late."

"I noticed that Gina seemed quite out of sorts today."

"Yes, and I must admit I feel rather uneasy about her. There's something here that I cannot understand at all, and I care for the girl. Owiński is perpetually lost in thought; he's a man you cannot rely upon. He strikes me as someone who would be deaf to any arguments, any reproaches. He is a typical poet."

"Then it may be that Gina is mistaken in avoiding marriage with him."

"Marriage? That would be a fine thing! She is surely affluent enough to do without it. Marriage!" she added, not without a touch of pride. "What use was it in Imszański's case, I wonder?"

She briefly glanced at a mirror hanging opposite her bed and then swiftly surveyed me from head to foot. The comparison between us must have been agreeable, for she immediately became more cheerful and friendly.

"My dear Miss Janina, Gina's nature is far too artistic for marriage. No one with her painting abilities would ever consider making a husband of her sweetheart. Pardon me; the idea is absolutely out of the question. Look at those flowers; how gracefully she has portrayed them!"

"They are indeed exquisite. But did you notice how keenly interested Owiński was in what you were saying about marriage last Thursday?"

"Yes, oh yes, I remember. But I can't imagine he is contemplating marrying anyone else. No, that is surely impossible."

She was instantly in a state of great excitement.

"Consider this: now that marriage is nothing more than a contract, ensuring the wife board and lodging for herself and offspring, and providing the husband with a permanent companion always at home and alert; now that a bachelor cannot embark on matrimony until he has achieved a position in the world, making an unmarried man who is not bald seem like a contradiction in terms—marriage, in principle, equates to the same as prostitution, with each particular aspect being even more unsettling."

"I'm afraid I don't quite follow your line of thought."

"Why, the concept is as crystal clear as it can be. A courtesan engages in a temporary bargain, and if extended, she always reserves complete liberty of action, intervals of freedom, and the power to break free whenever she pleases. In contrast, the 'honest woman' makes a lifelong agreement with no hope of liberation, especially considering that a divorced woman is negatively viewed by her 'honest' sisters. Even a common courtesan, residing in a house of ill fame, has her 'Alphonse'—someone with whom she can express sincere, true, and unselfish love. This is something the average honest woman cannot allow herself without the imminent risk of losing her right to alimony. Now, as for the moral distinction, it lies in this: one possesses only one husband, along with society's respect, while the other has many and is scorned. I fail to see any logical connection between a woman having multiple lovers and her obligation to respect the rights of humanity. Moreover, the police oversee the streetwalker's health, but who tends to the wife contaminated by her own husband? The former may die of anything; the latter, the honest woman, may succumb in childbirth if married, or if not—if she lacks a portion and cannot have a husband—she may perish from any cause.

Abolitionists organize congresses, publish books and pamphlets, establish philanthropic institutions, shelters, Christian associations to rehabilitate fallen women, and youth leagues to protect their purity during school years. All this, for what purpose? So that a common doctor, not the police, oversees the street girl's health; a few foolish females are confined not to brothels but to sewing rooms, and some women must teach their husbands things the latter have yet to learn! And all this in the interest of 'coming generations!' It's an empty phrase. Isn't it all rather ridiculous?"

She laughed, but her words pained me deeply.

"But then, instead of this, are we to do nothing?"

"Not at all. Let's establish homes and shelters, not for the women but for the children whose mothers are unable to care for them. And as for the so-called ignominy, let it remain; but we should mock it. Allow me to add," she continued in a more earnest tone, "that loosening, to the extent possible, all artificial bonds is a far easier and more natural task than tightening them. Both paths lead to the same goal—with the difference that in one case, the goal signifies freedom, and in the other, slavery."

As she spoke, I recalled what Witold had shared with me about her.

She abruptly broke off. "Oh, let's join the company! What will they think of a hostess who neglects her guests so!"

In the drawing-room, Owiński had not yet made his appearance. Gina, as beautiful as a portrait by some Old Master, reclined silently in an rose-colored easy-chair.

Imszański shot a glance and a faint smile at Madame Wildenhoff and offered me his arm to go in to supper.

Whoever it was—Amiel, I think—who maintained that women do not like to be analyzed was wrong. It is men who dislike such analysis.

Why does a woman rarely fall in love with a man inferior to herself? Because she wants to be loved for all that is in her. And from there stems the grievance, not less distasteful than groundless, that men do not see women as having minds as well as bodies. A man is quite satisfied if the woman acknowledges his superiority over her.

Those whom I like best are not those who attract me the most, but those who can comprehend and realize my whole power of attraction. That is why I dislike hearing Imszański babble, in a superficial and general manner, about the excellence of my nature, not knowing in what it consists and unable to grasp it.

And that is also why I have a liking for Wiążewski and a wish that he could find it in his heart to love me.

Spring is approaching. The hot sun hangs overhead, accompanied by a refreshing breeze. I feel exuberant, playful, and brimming with vitality. I could embrace the first person I encounter on the street! To be loved by someone, that is my longing. I might feel less dreadfully alone and disconnected from everything in the world—I would sacrifice many years of my life. Lord! If only someone would kiss me, now!—But not one of those. Oh, not one of them!

So many years have passed since that parting, never to fade from my mind! Yes, he was the only man I could have ever loved. How quickly it all passed away, and how completely it all came to an end! Strange—a fragment of life.

And now that happiness sleeps, beneath the flowery veils of many a past and gone springtime. Such a spring! And in my heart and life, all is so blank and dismal!

I have lived but a short time, a very short time; yet, despite that, I've gathered many fair flowers of memory! If only I could remember them all—all of them—then life would still be bearable.

And as I go on, I am ever closer and closer to life, wading along its foaming and tempestuous current. But in vain, I try to plunge into its waves and moisten these parched lips, as if traversing a sea of quicksilver whose dry metallic drops turn into liquid dust when touched.

Yet I have to wait—to wait—for something else, something akin to spring with its enchantment and sunshine. To wait for a marvel, a prodigy, a miracle that is to come!

With Gina and Owiński, I was leaving a coffeehouse. In front of us, surrounded by several men, there walked a woman, rather thickset, not tall, wearing a short-skirted, brightly colored dress and a wide-brimmed hat of a vivid hue. She moved slowly, with an undulating motion of the hips, turning now to the right, now to the left, now behind her, chatting with lively interest, her hands nimble with gestures like those of a flower-girl offering bouquets. We glimpsed her profile—long lashes and a short, straight nose. There seemed to be some enchantment emanating from that figure.

"A *coquette*?" I asked Gina.

She looked at her and nodded, with a somber expression.

We had been discussing love earlier. She resumed the topic where I had interrupted her.

"Ah, but I am not telling you it is absolute bliss. No. Love only intensifies all things, joy and pain alike. Love is an exceedingly powerful stimulant, strengthening all aspects of life. And when all its colors are suddenly brightened, life becomes like some magical fairy tale, an eternal Divine Vision of life."

Owiński, lost in his musings, was not paying attention, even though Gina was speaking especially for him. The golden fire in her eyes faded when she realized this.

"We ourselves are alone at fault; it is we who have brought about that immense misery, the fiery pain of which is now eating our hearts out. For every time we have turned a man away from us, every denial of the lips that belied the pulsing of the blood is a sin against Life. Every such night, when those who craved love and went urequited, but were perforce obliged to purchase it with gold, is a sin against Life—of which *we* are guilty.

"And therefore, we should all—like consecrated priestesses—go forth: go forth to suffering and to shame, with the laughter of Spring, and its cry *Evoë!*[23] love for love, joy for joy, pain for pain,—welling up from our hearts!"

"But why then pain?"

"I do not know; but so it has to be. Surely you feel that intense joy is not to be purchased without intense pain."

Owiński, looking down the long vista of the street, took not the slightest interest in what she was saying. Gina became silent; it may be that a feeling of shame had come upon her.

The strangely bewitching woman had stopped, coming to a sudden standstill to take leave of some of her companions. Her laughter resounded through the brightly lit, deserted street, with all the effrontery and witchery of Life itself.

Half-consciously, Owiński turned towards her, and so did we; a breath of the coming spring seemed to blow in our direction thence.

"Is she to your taste?" Gina asked her fiancé, with a curiosity in her tone of voice that she strove to make light of.

"What did you say?—oh, I don't know, didn't see her," he returned, daydreaming as usual.

Wishing to please her, he again turned round to look; but the whole company had already disappeared in the doorway of a neighboring restaurant.

Gina took his arm, with a gesture of famished and baffled desire. Laying her head on the sleeve of his great-coat, she brushed a wisp of hair from her cheek.

"No," she said to me in an undertone; "no, I cannot tell; I myself am ignorant of the end for which suffering exists; why must there always be suffering?"

Still Owiński heard not one word we said; so we could converse quite freely. For my part, I could not love a man so continually lost in thought.

"Seldom have I happened upon a type in such sharp contrast to all that I am," she continued, alluding to the woman we had just seen.

Far down in Gina's eyes, whose nervous energy was tired and worn out—somewhere very deep down—there shone a livid gleam of disquiet.

She gazed searchingly at her fiancé, but there was no change in the expression of his face. After a time, he was aware that her glance was upon him; then he bent forward to her, and, stroking her glove, said smiling:

"What is the matter with you, Gina?"

"Nothing—only love for you," she whispered.

Afterwards, we sat with Madame Wildenhoff almost until dawn.

"What's to be done? If he loves her no longer, he cannot be forced to stay with her," said Pani Lola to me, speaking of Owiński, of course. "Changes in feeling have nothing in common with ethics and a sense of duty." And so on, and so on.

Gina approached us presently.

"Tomorrow I'll be living on my own," she informed us. "I'm currently in such a state that I can't bear anyone, not even such an amiable person as Idalia. She will occupy my studio, which she likes very much, and the room she used to rent will now be available. I would greatly appreciate finding another tenant for her."

Madame Wildenhoff turned to me directly with these unexpected words:

"Wouldn't you like to share lodgings with Idalia? She plays so beautifully, and that family life must, I fancy, bore you by now."

It then crossed my mind that Madame Wildenhoff's intention was to separate me from Imszański! Was I right? Possibly.

"I shall think it over," I responded in a pleasant tone. "Though indeed I enjoy just as much listening to Marta play."

Staying up all night almost every forty-eight hours or so exhausts me beyond measure. They—that is, all the others—have nothing to do; they rise at noon, and enjoy plenty of money and leisure, and their greatest pleasure is engaging in endless discussions about the deepest problems of existence. But for me, what with battling with sleep in the morning, walking a considerable distance to my office through mud and slush, and sitting motionless at my desk for many hours, those nights burden me with fatigue that is hard to bear. I have, it is true, a sturdy frame: but such a lifestyle would wear it out eventually.

I am weary and miserable, and from time to time, I feel almost distracted. My state is like that of someone who has an appointment and waits, waits, waits, through the hours and through the years, although the time allotted to keep it has long since passed by. I experience the same fever of impatience, the same clutching at my heart when, in my delusion, I think I can at last hear his footsteps; the same chill of terror when, for an instant, I think he will never come.

All this is very banal, very "sentimental." Yes, I know, I know. But now and then, it is simply beyond my power to keep it down; it's simply overwhelming. I wonder if my time for meeting the one I would fall in love with has already fled into the past long ago?!

But no; it has come, that time has come! It came yesterday. I had already felt it in the air for many days; it was in Marta's eyes; my own heart told me. And while I yearned for it constantly, I feared it like a sentence of death.

Having returned long after Marta had fallen asleep, he noticed that there was a light in my room and tapped gently. I did not answer; nevertheless, he came in.

"How late you have stayed up reading!" he said in a whisper. And then, seating himself on the couch beside me, he remained silent.

Covering my eyes with my hands, I let my head droop as low as to his knees, and in an instant was possessed with a mad, frenzied effervescence of expectancy. I shivered all over as if with chills and fever, then shook all over with soundless laughter. Something was leaping up in my breast, palpitating in my very throat, in my brain, in my hands that were covering my eyes. Had this unparalleled excitement lasted but one moment more I should have cried out aloud with terror and agony.

Then, in an instant, I grew quiet, overwhelmed with a sense of sudden numbness, and I let my head droop even lower. Witold bent over me, kissing my hair and shoulders. Then, he raised my head, showering kisses on my eyes, mouth, and throat.

Not one word of love did we speak. Long before, we had understood each other, but a thousand thoughts rushed through my brain. He bent his marvelously beautiful head down to my knees, whispering a few strange, inaudible words—words of incantation, words of magic. He could afford to be humble, for he was like a king who knows how mighty he is and how supreme. Then his lips grew very red, as if on fire.

All at once, I shook myself free with a hissing intake of breath and gently extricated myself from his embrace.

"What, my Queen of the Icy Caverns!" he said in sport, his eyes fixed upon mine. "Has some thought of death come to make you afraid?"

"No; I was thinking of Marta."

His bantering humor left him at once.

"Oh! for once in our lives, surely we might learn to think only of ourselves," he said, and his tone showed he was vexed with me.

"And have you found that lesson so very hard to learn?"

"That's unkind of you," he whispered, closing my mouth with a kiss.

"And now I have no more love left, not even for my husband. Not that I love another, not that Witold has made me suffer torments beyond endurance. No: I am merely unable to feel anything else in the world save pain. The very thought of him is torture."

As she spoke, I bowed my head very low.

"It may be that there is some world in which Kant's 'categories' do not hold, where we are out of Space, out of Time. I believe it is so. Sometimes space does not exist for me: I have the power to see all those he has loved with him in one place. There are moments, too, when time does not exist for me: I can see them all together in one instant—both those that have been and those that are to be; yes, those that are to be, Janka."

From under her brows, she threw me a questioning glance and went on.

"But I can see, I can fancy nothing, save under the mental form of Pain. Yes, and I have thus discovered a new 'category'!"

It was difficult to say why, just at that moment, I remembered Wielołęski and his discovery that land-owning was also a "category," and this put me in a humor of pleasantry that it was not easy to shake off.

"Looked at through this prism of Pain," she continued, "the sun itself is black, the most superb flowers in the Red Garden turn to tongues of flame, and the cistern filled with flowers of bliss changes into an infinite, infinite ocean of blood."

She looked around and shuddered.

"Pray, Janka, do not go to bed tonight; do not leave me alone during the dark hours. Truly, I cannot remember when he went out. I think he was not at home at all today."

"Yes, he was; he dined with us."

She passed her hand over her brow.

"You are right, but it doesn't matter. At any rate, he will not be here until morning. Janka, do not sleep in your room!"

By this time, it is impossible for me to endure the sight of Marta. She fills me with such mystic awe that I am ready to shriek aloud from dread of her. I feel as though I were the cause of all her afflictions, as if it were I who has marred her life. Her eyes hurt me—those great dark-blue, sorrowful eyes. But all the same, it must make no difference to her; to her who…

On returning from the office, I stepped into Madame Wildenhoff's, to see about the room Gina spoke of. At any price, I must get away from here. I never want to see either her or him anymore.

Madame Wildenhoff was a little paler than her usual; she looked out of sorts and complained that her head ached. I understood that something had gone wrong between him and her. And again, my heart was crushed with fear. Only when I looked at her did I remember that she likewise... I had, for the time being, entirely forgotten that fact. My first impulse was to flee her, but Madame Wildenhoff retained me against my will. She, I think, has not made any definite guess, but the other!

"I must confess to you," she began, "that all I have made you think of me is untrue—a mask of mine, a mannerism, an empty theory. All women are at their heart's core exactly alike; during all their life, they follow one thing alone and perish in pursuit of it."

"You mean love?" I questioned, trying clumsily to feign indifference.

"Yes. That is the one thing. It is our fate; if not the first thing that we pursue, it is always the last that we give up. There is no help for it—none. We may be all our life forcing upon ourselves the conviction that we have the same rights as men and are capable of bearing the same amount of liberty as they; but there must come a moment when, for that one true love, we most willingly give up all its counterfeits."

"But you have, Madame, the comfort to know that men too are liable to a similar reaction. When quite sated with freedom, the very greatest profligates will settle down to married life."

"Only for a short while, and then they begin all over again and return to their favorite pastime. Why, take Imszański, for instance; you surely know him well."

My face flushed up as red as fire, but I undauntedly raised my eyes to hers. She, on encountering my gaze, blushed, too. Once more I felt an uneasy flutter at my heart.

She burst into a sudden transport.

"I love, I love, and without any return! Oh, how unlike me, is it not?"

Whereupon she laughed hysterically, and then shed tears, tearing at her handkerchief with her teeth. She was waiting for me to ask her some questions, so that she might be able to confide her sorrows in me. I thought I should soon likely go mad.

At last, Gina came in. She took me to Idalia, a fairly well-known pianist, who returned here from Paris a year before.

The room was very much to my taste; so was Idalia. There, all is tranquil and artistic. There I find nothing of that monstrous life that hurts me so—that lie which I feel here in my eyes as they look, in my mouth as it speaks!

Now I have left the Imszańskis for good. Even for my nature, life with them was too exquisite a torment.

Marta, according to her custom, has understood everything but let nothing come to her as a surprise. Nor has she in any way altered her behavior towards me.

When I told her it was too far for me to go from her house to the office, she never asked why, during close upon three years, I had not noticed the distance. She appears not to know that I am aware she has no more trust in me.

When, for the last time, I entered my room, in which there was but little change (for only a few of my things had been brought to their flat), I burst out crying. Marta stood by my side, grave and mournful.

Later, too, at the moment of my departure, there came to me a horrible pain of unbounded bewilderment, that took me, so to speak, suddenly by the throat. All this was, I thought, so heart-rending, so incomprehensible!

Imszański was speaking to the porter who helped the man-servant to take my things downstairs. Then I asked

Marta: "Don't you—don't you think it would be better for me to die now, this instant?"

A smile dawned on her face, which she averted to hide it.

"No," she said; "there is no need. Nothing comes to me unexpectedly now. And latterly I have found an enemy—in myself anyway."

Quietly, daintily, she kissed me on the lips, and then, with a gracious gesture, gave her hand to Imszański, who was going out to take me to my new abode.

I sit for a long time, spending the evening with Imszański. And I enjoy myself. Although I do not for one instant forget her, that graceful melancholy woman, who now is wandering through the magnificent apartments of her lonely dwelling, always awaiting him, though she knows he will not come, and at the slightest noise rushing to the ante-chamber, listening with her ear close against the door, and her brain on fire with excitement. But the billows of undisturbed stillness are beating all around her. And then she goes back to her rooms, and seats herself upon an easy-chair, and again upon a lounge, trying to fall asleep; and to keep herself from sobbing aloud, she bites her fingers hard. And in a little while she goes once again and listens at the ante-chamber door. For now, I am no longer by her side; now she is quite, quite alone; and so cruelly abandoned!

Not for an instant do I forget all this; and yet I enjoy myself. The faint bitterness of this tragedy gives, I suppose, an additional flavor to our amorous and delightful dalliance.

Witold would prefer not to speak of the subject, which I nevertheless bring forward again and again.

"But tell me now, how could you behave with such abominable baseness, forcing yourself into Marta's life so? For you married her under downright compulsion: I well remember that she resisted with all her might. Were you at the time really in love with her?"

"She attracted me extremely, and I was puzzled by her intense regard for chastity. Never before had I encountered any woman with the instinct developed to such an extent. And I was then in a romantic, an idealistic, a Platonic mood, with which Marta harmonized perfectly."

"Well, and how was it that this mood of yours came to alter so quickly?"

"I found Marta just a little disappointing, and even at the time when I married her, I was quite sure that she could not satisfy me for long. All that alluring mystery of her ascetic philosophy of life merely stemmed from anemia and poverty of temperament."

"Witold! Witold! Do go back to her again. Remember; I shall never love you as she does."

"No, I will not; I will not," and he gathered me in his arms. "I will not leave you, nor would I, even if you came to hate me. Besides: what, in this whole affair, has pained Marta most? Why, it is your leaving us. She is always sitting in your room, and she very often talks of you and wonders why you don't come."

I believed that all Witold had said was but a part of Marta's behavior, studiously correct in regard to him: but I have received a letter from her today.

"Come to me, Janka, come! Do not bear me more ill-will than I bear to you. Remember that everything in our relations is still just as it was before. The memories are too deep-rooted; I cannot… Once I loved you even more than…

"I await you. M."

I shall go to her tomorrow.

She received me, dressed in a black dressing-gown with grey borders and a silver fringe. I found it hard to conceal the painful impression that I felt. We talked together in a friendly way for about an hour.

With some air of mystery, she explained to me the idea she had of fitting up a bedchamber entirely in mourning. "It might be made quite ornamental. The walls hung with crepe, the furniture of black wood, upholstered with white plush, crosses of silver and of ebony, standing and suspended chandeliers of silver, a profusion of such flowers as are used to dress a catafalque, a large table in the center, covered with a black cloth. And the bedchamber lit with candles only."

She then showed me an album bound in black leather, with a silver cross that stood out in relief on the cover.

With an embarrassed smile, she explained its contents to me.

"Here I have placed all Witold's loves, in chronological order," she said, and the very sound of his name made her blush hotly. "The number looks very great indeed, but this is because I have in many cases several portraits of the same person."

I surveyed it for a while, fascinated and entranced by these faces, each of a distinct type—some laughing, some serious, some poignant, others comical, exotic, or ordinary. They were full of fire or ethereal-looking, many adorned in peculiar attire or striking voluptuous poses, stretching out their semi-nude limbs with serpent-like grace. All of them surrounded by exotic splendor. And then there were exquisite women, very refined in their British stiffness, dressed in the sexless elegance of tailor-made attire—simple but striking. A myriad, chaotic assembly representing various styles and nationalities, including a quite sensual African woman, undoubtedly a singer in some music hall.

"Since you've been away," she said, "it has been a habit of mine to pore over this album. Those different faces remind me of the different periods of my life. I possess but few from the old times of Witold's love-making, but of those he loved since he married, not one is absent here. Some of them I purchased myself."

"That," I observed, "was a former habit of yours. I remember well how, as a girl, you preferred making collections of post-cards with photographs of handsome actresses."

"Oh, but that was quite different," she replied with a shake of the head. "I find such pleasure in gloating over this collection!"

"Yes, the pleasure you take in self-inflicted torture!"

"No, not even that. You see, I gaze at those beautiful faces, those full red voluptuous mouths, those white rounded shoulders, so pleasantly smooth and soft. I look through the garments and see the color of the flesh beneath, and each of these women I imagine delirious, swooning in his arms. So, I feed my mind with the thought of their delight in him—or perhaps (I am not quite sure which) of his delight in them!"

Her nostrils were quivering. She settled herself in her soft-cushioned seat and closed her eyelids; they were red with tears.

On one of the first pages of the album, I found Maria Wielołęska, clad as an Algerian girl, blithe and beguiling, and far better-looking than in reality. Towards the end, there were about a dozen photographs of Madame Wildenhoff and one—a small one—of that French actress whom we had seen at the Lipka. The thought flashed upon me—a very unflattering one assuredly—that she had already placed me there too. Still, sitting as I was by Marta's side, I could not possibly look at the last page. Besides, she herself held the album and showed me no photographs after those of Madame Wildenhoff and the French actress.

The same thought occurred to us both at once, casting over us the shadow of a moody silence.

She laid her head on my bosom and closed her eyes with an expression of utmost fatigue.

"Don't go on like that," I said to her soothingly. "That way madness lies, and you might easily get there."

"Oh, that is very likely. Indeed, I wish I may. Oh, to lose memory, consciousness, and all feeling!" And then: "For I am everlastingly wringing my own heart, Janka!" she added, very sorrowfully.

Silently, I stroked her long, disheveled hair, and all the while, with tender craving and emotional entrancement, my mind kept going to Witold.

"Are you my husband's paramour by now?"

It was with some surprise that I was aware the question evoked in me a reaction of outraged dignity. But I choked down the feeling, and unembarrassed, though with downcast eyes, I answered, in a low voice:

"No, not as yet."

"That is better. You may then presently become his wife."

Her mouth was slightly twitching. She has that most unpleasant habit of melting with compassion over her own woes.

"Only, please, Marta, not death! Let's not talk about death!"

"I am in a very bad way."

"The idea! You always have been so terribly afraid to die; you told me so. Do you remember?"

"Oh, but it's an entirely different matter now! Afraid of death, me? No, I yearn for it with the deepest longing of my wretched heart. Yes, I crave it so that you may become his wife, that you may personally delve into the depths of the torments I've endured and bask (as I am doing) in the radiant beams of the bliss they provide. May you, like me, drink in the delight by the cupful, brimming over! Even more, may you indulge in wormwood until you overflow with it! Be suffocated with the mortal scent of his flowers—imbibe their fragrant delight and the poisonous steam of them, even to agony, even to death! May I be avenged when you are compelled to yield him up to another! And may the knowledge that even death itself is no sufficient expiation make the bitterness of your last hour even more bitter. Oh, God!"

She hid her face in her hands, trembling violently with the intensity of her spasmodic outburst. Finally, she fell on her knees before me, covering my hands with burning-hot kisses.

"No, Janka, these words of mine are not true; they are lies—lies! There is no longer any hatred at all, nor any thirst for vengeance. I love you! I shall die so that you may be happy—in his Red Garden—and that he too may be happy by your side. Don't you believe me? Won't you look into my heart? My only wish is for your happiness: beyond this, I have no wish whatsoever. I humble myself at your feet like this, see! and bless you for taking away from me what is dearer than life itself; for pouring into the cistern of my bliss the last drop of that nectar which inebriates unto death. I love you. Wasn't it Christ who commanded us to love our enemies. Hear me! I am dying so that you may be happy with him. I wish you all happiness. I want to receive death at your hands—your beautiful hands, so soft to caress. I would not have you feel any twinge of remorse; I wish you could kill me and yet not know that my death has cleared the way for your triumphal chariot. Oh, Janka! be happy!"

Her head fell back; her eyes closed tightly, and her teeth were clenched, showing between her half-open lips.

"Slay me, oh, slay me!"

Now she has fainted. I lift her up and lay her limp and seemingly lifeless body on a couch.

The purple chamber grows dark in the gathering twilight.

III
A HYMN TO LOVE

"I anticipate your arrival in a day or two, so this letter will likely remain unsent. I'm writing solely for the pleasure of having this evening to myself with you in mind. And if I do put these words on paper, it's for my own sake.

It's a splendid autumn evening. I yearn to be in your company, my dear, my one and only!

The earth is cloaked in darkness, the sky painted in shades of blue, and the night is descending. Not long ago, Idalia handed me a letter from you, and now I find myself in a mood of tenderness. I won't scold you for your candid expression of desires in your naturalistic manner. There are moments when I can forgive anything. I want to demonstrate my love for you, sincerely and deeply. The days of my discontent, the days of my dark anxieties, have given way, and the days of bright vision have arrived. Just this morning, I was telling Idalia that I'd advise her against falling in love because I am so far gone that I cannot imagine myself capable of loving anyone but you.

I would be so much better for you if I weren't afraid. Ever since you made your confession, I fear you might gain the upper hand. In matters of love, I don't believe two can be on equal footing. And if I surrender even a small part of my rights to you, you exhibit no generosity; instead, you revel in my self-abasement as if it were utter degradation. Witold, show a bit of generosity; permit me a moment of respite from this perpetual vigil over myself. Let me love you in peace, even if only for a short while.

Again and again, I'm haunted by the painful thought that, just like last time, the joy of our reunion won't compensate for the ache of separation. I also suspect that you might have come today but chose not to, claiming ignorance as you did before. I harbor no reproach, but I'm slightly piqued and may, once again, distance myself as I did last spring. Perhaps this will help you appreciate how congenial, clever, and incomparable I am.

There's no denying it: you're more in love with me than I am with you. I'm being forthright about it because it's not entirely accurate. Now, I'm about to share a crucial point that I haven't made explicitly clear before, and I need a direct response from you. So, pay attention! We could potentially love each other equally, but I love you less. Why? Because you don't fret in the slightest about my love—neither about your admitted actions nor, more importantly, about your current disposition. You've done what you've done, and you feel as you feel. You find honesty more convenient than concealment. As a result, I'm constantly maintaining the intensity of your love, suppressing my feelings, and not revealing what I truly feel. This is unjust. You once told me, 'Never let me gain the upper hand, for I would make a slave of you. As soon as Marta became my slave, I ceased to love her.' In response, I decided to maintain my position of superiority, becoming more secretive and less natural. I carefully hid away any weakness, abasement, or spiritual poverty—the eternal feminine—keeping it to myself alone to ensure our love had a longer lifespan. This should concern you as much as it does me. If I were to tell you not to press your cheek against my dress or not to humble yourself before me because I cannot love where I do not honor, you would start sulking and accuse me, like a cross and sullen child, of being the one who loves less. In my opinion, preserving our mutual love is a joint responsibility. It's like an altar on which both of us should sacrifice absolute sincerity, especially concerning passing moods, and more specifically those implying self-abasement. We must play a role, wear a mask, and keep any grievances that might diminish one in the eyes of the other strictly to ourselves. So, I ask you, who knows this well from your own experiences: am I right or not? If I am, then, do you plan to make me love you as much as you love me, or are you willing to lower the level of your love to match mine? In other words, will you bear the burden of constant vigilance with me, or do you deliberately agree to let me set it aside? Answer me this. And please don't forget it in ten minutes. Despite it all, I love you very much.

J. D."

Witold just returned yesterday. He attended a large shooting event in Kłosów, a commitment he had to fulfill to demonstrate his amicable ties with Janusz, thereby putting an end to the rumors circulating among the local gentry about his supposed separation from Marta. I once prohibited Janusz from hunting hares; that's long forgotten now, and he's impressing everyone with his newfound skill as a marksman. The past is the past!

In the past few years, which haven't had any noticeable impact on Witold, Janusz has undergone a radical transformation. He married a "country girl," gained weight, became ruddy and commonplace, and now boasts four sons, with a fifth one on the way, according to the news Witold brings. The former untamed essence of his nature only emerges during occasional town visits when he revels and carouses vigorously, usually in Witold's company.

Marta has been in Germany for about six months, receiving treatment at a nervous patients' sanatorium. She is not allowed to send or receive letters, but sporadic updates from the doctor indicate her improving condition, suggesting a return home shortly. The doctor politely mentions that she always longs for her husband and son. The son is being raised alongside Janusz's boys, benefiting from the healthy country air.

I took a brief vacation this summer, spending most of the time in town with Witold, leading a quasi-domestic life. In my case, he seems particularly concerned about maintaining appearances. I wonder why he never cared about them during his past involvement with Madame Wildenhoff. Perhaps, by being meticulous now, he intends to emphasize how much he values me.

He read my letter without offering any comments, abruptly switching to recounting an incident from the shooting party. Then, he proceeded to lavish me with caresses and kisses, expressing how much he had missed me.

"But answer my question, Witold," I insisted.

"How can I? I don't know," he replied, ardently kissing my inquisitive eyes.

"Janka, isn't this the best answer of all?" he added. He's always like that; my glances set us apart, while his kisses bring us together.

Yet, I am wrestling, ensnared in the grip of my love, much like a kite soaring above the clouds wrestles with the string held by a playful boy.

Idalia doesn't mind having company at her place, where I've encountered various personalities from the artistic world. Wiążewski may not appreciate the term "Bohemianism," but despite this, he willingly joins us to "observe."

"Take a good look at all those men," he remarks. "Mostly ill-shaped, ill-favored, sitting in corners, smoking cigarettes, and paying no attention to whether ladies are present or not. Skeptical and pessimistic, with an exaggerated view of everything, deadly serious about their convictions. That's the type of men I find most abhorrent. If intelligent, they become narrow-minded; if dull, utterly impossible in society. Have you noticed that the greatest fool, as long as he has no convictions of his own, can be a very nice, gentlemanly fellow."

"And what about the women?"

"They are less unbearable. They don't discuss feminism, disapprove of women's emancipation, and, best of all, effectively practice it. They possess a lot of intuition, but luckily, not a grain of conscious experience."

"Whom do you like best of all?"

"Miss Janina Dernowicz."

"I was asking about artists; I am not one."

"Ah, I see. Artists? The prettiest is Miss Wartosławska, whom I've known for a good while. But currently, she doesn't look as well as usual. Why isn't Owiński accompanying her now?"

"Owiński?" I hesitated for a moment. Then, "Well, the engagement has been broken off for a month," I said.

"Has it? Yes, I had heard something about his being engaged to someone, but thought it was mere gossip. Why, he seemed to be a very passive sort of fellow and bore the yoke meekly enough."

"I don't know who is responsible for what has taken place."

"Oh, you have but to look at her, and you can't help guessing. Besides, women always love longer and more deeply. It is through love that they attain their highest degree of culture; and I must acknowledge that, so far as culture goes, they have outstripped men; a woman's instinct stands higher than the wisdom of a man."

"Why, Stefan, from where have you got this attitude of benevolent optimism towards woman?"

"Of tragical pessimism, I should say," he answered, cheerfully, but then was lost in contemplation.

How am I to know? Very likely this also is love. And a good thing, too, that it came to me: I was so lonely then and so crushed with longing!

Now and then I enjoy emotions of superhuman delight, of ecstatic bewilderment. And then again there flutter about me, like black moths, certain bitter self-reproaches for the past, and maddening apprehensions as to the future,—Really, it is too ridiculous! As if there could be anything worse than the sepulchral monotony of my life, as it formerly was!

And yet I know—I know!—that this is not happiness: that this romantic adventure of mine will have no morrow.

Put an end to it? I cannot; for just now the man is as necessary to me as the air I breathe. But sometime or other I shall not love him anymore; and then I shall hold it as a sacred duty to pay him for his deeds in the past by my future conduct.

And she, this my poor love! stands here, gazing with eyes full of frantic terror about her end, that will and must come someday!

The keynote in the tragedy of woman's life is the fact that her need for permanent love stands in contradiction with men's instincts and with their interests. Wiążewski calls this her "higher culture." I think that Schopenhauer's justification of this need as simply a case of design in nature is far more convincing.[24] For how can we see any superiority in an instinct that we find equally developed in the most refined ladylove with her deep emotions, and in the average middle-class woman, all given up to passivity and routine?

After Owiński had engaged himself to a new fiancée, he would still, in the beginning, come at times and call upon Gina.

She would receive him with a smiling face and serene looks, and endeavor to delude him into thinking that no change had taken place, and that if he said he had come back to her, she would be neither surprised nor dismayed. She would talk about things which had interested them both; about her paintings and his poems. Together they read books, treating of the Beautiful, and Life, and Love. Once he said that he could not come to see her the next day, as his intended was to arrive in town; she took it as quietly as if he had announced his mother's or his sister's arrival. But though they still called each other by their Christian names, they no longer kissed, not even at parting.

On one occasion, she requested him to recite one of his poems, a request to which he always willingly acceded. She listened, adapting to each changing phrase of his mind, as she had done in the past, and following every flash of his eye. Now, there were many of his works with which she was not familiar; formerly, she had been the first to read anything he wrote. With a composed and tranquil demeanor, she listened even to the love-song written for "the other." Of course, they were the output of the reaction that had set in: the magic power of innocence; the first confession of love from the untouched lips of one ignorant of life; the return of his springtime, of his youth, of his ideals. Gina exhibited great self-control. At the end of one such poem, she handed him a love-song from the old times, written three years before and under her enchantment. And he read this one aloud as he had read the others, showing a fire that, alas, was too evidently out of all connection with the object that had once inspired them.

Like a tune deeply ingrained in memory from bygone days, the words immediately brought all the past before her: it rose up, plainly visible to her mind's eye. The vision was agonizing, and the dismay of it made her raise her hands to her throat, as if to prevent the outburst of lamentation that now tore her bosom, as if she had been a feeble child, long and unjustly ill-treated. She wept like one distraught, even forgetting that he was present and only aware that all her universe had given way, was broken to pieces, crumbled to dust, annihilated.

Someone embraced her tenderly, smoothing her hair and planting a kiss on her moist, red, tear-swollen eyes. She felt it, and this gesture, meant to comfort her, seemed harder for her to bear than anything else. It was a kiss of pure sympathy for suffering, of mere humanity, a final farewell kiss.

The anguish she felt stifled her, making it difficult for her to breathe, until her pain erupted in a tempest of weeping. Then, as if in a nightmare, she heard his footsteps moving farther and farther away, accompanied by the sound of the door closing behind him. She knew it was closing on him forever; she knew he would not return.

There came a time when she crawled to his feet, like some poor creature that its master had driven away. No longer welcome in his house, she lingered in coffee-houses and on the street, incessantly sending him letters. Wherever he went, he was doomed to encounter that face, pale as a specter, and those eyes, reproachful and full of pleading!

Now Owiński greets her distantly, treating her like a mere acquaintance. He gives no response to any of her letters and no longer visits people if there's a chance of encountering her.

When I gaze at Gina, Marta immediately comes to my mind.

Once, I believed I had gained the knowledge that there is neither good nor evil.

Nevertheless, there is a feeling in my heart—a persistently silly feeling—that all that has happened is evil, most evil, whereas it might just as well have been good. An extraneous otherness; circumstances, or perhaps dispositions, make all the difference.

Yes, but I continually see those eyes—those pure dark-blue eyes that didn't deserve the agony she has suffered—and the curve of that mouth, her tiny crimson mouth, hardened with pain and always ready to burst into lamentations.

She sometimes appears to me as a fiend, whom I hate for her obstinate will to suffer, for the childish and insensate whim of posing as a victim, for her attitudes and her love to gloat over herself. She comes with black wings and fluttering white hands; with a beggar's impudence, she opens her mourning gown and shows me her bosom; beneath her white transparent flesh, I can see her purple-colored heart. And she points to it. It is misery that has stained it so deep a red, filling it with red fire; for there is not a single drop of blood in it anymore.

And she delicately strokes that heart, savoring the moment with a sinister smile.

I am tormented by remorse!

To discern between good and evil is not particularly wise. That's why my ethical principles are of such primitive simplicity. My culture resides solely in my brain; the emotional part of me remains elemental and primitive, filled with foolish sentiment and scruples.

This is the reason I am so different from other women, whose predominant trait is the cultivation of their feelings.

Sometimes, when I see him from a distance, standing out from the crowd, splendid in shape and wonderful in beauty, I feel a sense of pride that he is mine—my own! Not a pet cat, dog, parrot, or canary, but a man of the world, tall, refined, in the prime of life. And this marvelous creature belongs to me. It's truly hard to realize this, and my brain whirls with pleasure at the mere thought of such possession.

When sitting by my side, he loses that charm of his, so extremely rare and valuable—the charm of aloofness. He is undoubtedly mine, my Witold. I know him well; I know him by heart. Always by fits and starts; incorrigible in his defects, which are exceedingly hard to bear; obstinate and childish; his mind consists of two or at most three strata, with the uppermost alone containing a little gold; and beneath this, you may root and dig all your life long, finding nothing but sand, and sand, and sand forever! But why do I always want to discover things and go deeper and deeper?

When he kisses, it is as if he were drinking the blood out of me. I turn pale, weak, and inert—ever more and more inert. In his arms, I melt, like a flower drooping and dying in the sun. I lack the strength even to raise my eyelids; it's as though the lashes grow together.

But—and this is an odd thing—I never yield beyond a certain point, not determined by any resolve or will of mine, but by instinct alone. A moment comes when there surges up within me, as it were, a cold and ironically smiling energy; with one gesture, I repel that creature full of intemperate desire, enchanting though he is in his thoughtless waywardness.

He always leaves humbled, vanquished, and concealing under the hearty kindness of a farewell kiss the gathering hostility of an everlasting antagonism.

Indeed, I have never yet been his "paramour," in any sense of the word used by Marta when she questioned me.

Yet, when victorious, I at times wish that I had been defeated. Truly, I cannot understand myself. But I do not even attempt to strive against this something within me that can even overcome the natural bent of my temperament.

It is conceivably the instinct of self-preservation, which has in woman, through the immemorial working of heredity, been turned in one and only one special direction, antagonistic to unchaste. The ideal woman would prefer death to what is called *shame*, would she not?

And I also possess this involuntary and automatic tendency, instinctive yet purposeful, and in me, it is only very partially blunted by the force of sober reason. But this explains well why my inclination towards emancipation has its source and finds its scope chiefly in the intellectual sphere.

Last evening, I spent some time in Gina's studio. I was glad she had asked me to come, for last night there was something or other at Witold's club, and I do not like to spend my evenings alone now. I fear my own thoughts, which are never so profound as in solitude and at night. This activity of my mind sometimes exceeds my limited strength to bear it. And when I note that there is some resemblance between myself and Marta, I again hear her prediction of vengeance ringing in my ears. There are moments when, oh, how weak, how very weak I feel!

Although I've known Gina for quite a while, our interactions always maintain a formal tone. When we encounter each other at a mutual friend's gathering, she keeps her demeanor almost distant. As a hostess, she not only displays courtesy but is also eager to extend it, and this difference in her behavior is quite noticeable. At home, she rarely appears gloomy, ensuring the conversation never falters. She enthusiastically shares her paintings, albums, new periodicals, and books, offering delicious black coffee and constantly moving about with a light and supple grace. Clad in a long dark gown with trailing skirts, adorned with gold earrings and a metallic belt, she navigates through the easels, canvases, and assorted stools in her studio with admired disorder. Tactfully, she avoids discussing herself, preferring to keep our conversation free from any shadow of gloom.

"Are you quite comfortable?" she inquires kindly. "Please don't stand on ceremony; sit down on this ottoman—very cozy, believe me. Let me put this skin under your head—the softest fur; as soft as silk. Now, isn't it nice to rest on?"

She fetches a tiny stand, placing a cup of coffee, tea-cakes, and a small glass within easy reach.

"Now, a little drop of liqueur; that will do nicely, won't it?"

In her studio, a beautiful soft red twilight prevails. The lamp, well shaded, glows in a corner upon a low table. The easels cast long-drawn, big, and grotesque black lines upon the upper parts of the walls. A glazed roof, forming the majority of the ceiling, resembles black velvet framed in white with pink flowers along the frames.

Gina, to some extent, imitates Costenoble.[25] The latest sketch she made for a large painting depicts a man, his head thrown back in a pose of fatuous triumph, while a woman at his feet, subtly delicate in attitude, suggests the coils of a writhing serpent.

The sketch as a whole is melodramatic and not very convincing. I prefer Gina as Gina, not as an artist.

I love gazing at her, sitting close to me, reclining in that big easy chair, her long white hands carelessly dangling from the arms, forming a beautiful and dainty picture.

"Would you come with me to a concert next Thursday?" she asks. "Ileska is reciting a poem by my ex-fiancé. He will be there, and so will she. I haven't seen her yet and would like to. There will also be piano and vocal music. Not a bad program."

"Of course, I'll be pleased, but have you considered..."

"Oh, don't worry, I'll manage. It can't make a great impression on me."

She smiles.

"I wouldn't have forced myself on you, but since Lola Wildenhoff's departure, I have no one but you for this service. I am easily upset now, and any lack of tact jars upon me."

"I thought you were pretty close with Idalia."

"Not at present. True, she is still, as she always was, discreet. But she has too much sentiment and sympathy—far too much, and that is annoying and mortifying. You, so tranquil, so quiet, so entirely unmoved, act on my nerves like a sedative. I can talk with you even more openly than with Lola."

"Oh, have you heard from her?"

"Yes, I received a letter. She's left the Riviera and is in Paris now, planning to spend the winter with her husband. Wildenhoff has won a significant amount of money at Monte Carlo, and they're both enjoying it, each in their own way."

"And how are her nerves?"

"In perfect condition. She left all her tears in the sea behind her. That woman has an uncommonly happy disposition."

After this, a brief but mournful pause ensued, interrupted by the entrance of Radłowski, a painter who had been her fellow student in Munich. He noticed that my complexion was notably unique and requested that I sit for my portrait.

Witold believes that, of all the women he's known, I am the most intelligent. Before meeting me, he had been ascending a ladder of emotions, with Marta forming the topmost rung. I seem to represent a synthesis of all his loves; I am simultaneously the most beloved, humanly speaking, and the most desired woman. He wouldn't have me any other way. However, I wish I could say the same about him.

Yet, I wouldn't exactly want him changed—rather transformed into another person. It seems that being as lack-brained as an animal isn't sufficient; one must also have some primitive instincts, some vigor. What I now crave irresistibly is matchless strength—the strength of a hurricane, a cyclone, some great natural force unleashed.

He enjoys discussing intellectual matters with me. "No one can understand my soul as well as you," he tells me. In silence, with eyes cast down, I listen to his platitudes, expressed in elaborately chosen words and in a non-commonplace manner. I ponder as I gaze upon him—on that perfectly shaped, sweet mouth, slightly faded; and those eyes, bright with the fever and melancholy of lassitude, full of the irresistible charm that surrounds all that is coming to an end, yet you wish it to remain as beautiful as only youth's dream can be. And it is then—when he has no inkling of what I feel—that I love him most of all.

Today, I felt sorry for him—for all those desires of his, destined to burn themselves out, never to be kindled again. Acting on an impulse, I went up to him, knelt with one knee upon his, put my hands around his head—wonderfully soft and velvet-like to feel. Then, turning his face up, I gazed into those enchanting, nebulous eyes and said laughingly:

"Oh, in Heaven's name, Witold, why must you talk about everything? You know well enough that this is not what you were made for, don't you? Pray remember that your one strong point is love."

And then, for the first time, I kissed him on the lips, not waiting to be kissed by him. He kissed me back, but the kiss was cool, brotherly.

"I regret," he observed, "that you show me so little of your beautiful soul and refuse to acknowledge mine to be of a kindred nature. Yet I understand so well your dreams of the Arctic plains that you possess, of your grottoes glimmering green in the Northern Lights; of your boundless and ever peacefully slumbering ocean! I am forever very near to you."

"That may be; but I always feel quite distant from you," I replied, attempting a bit of humor. Then I whispered in his ear, "Love my snows, for there are volcanoes seething beneath them."

Upon hearing these words, his mouth latched onto my neck, biting into my flesh with a kiss that gave me exquisite pain mingled with maddening delight. My eyelids closed, my lips parted, and I was on the verge of fainting. I felt his mouth on mine, sweet with the savor of withered roses. I drank the crimson wine of his kisses, and it was potent as death. The intoxication overwhelmed me.

However, there came an unsettling moment. Was it Death, or was it Life, that laid its cold hand upon my heart and regarded me with the eyes of wisdom? The revulsion freed me, tearing me from his close embrace. I hated him, for he didn't understand and was unwilling to let me go. Yet, had he left me then, I would have resented it and longed for him!

No, I will never be won by the graces of a young page with tawny eyelashes, nor by the refined softness and subtlety of any art. Strength alone can win me. Like a cat carrying off its little ones in its jaws, let Him carry me away; and wherever he may take me, there I shall go.

When we entered the concert hall, it was already full. Gina looked like a ghost. We spotted many people we knew, and several gentlemen came to present their respects. They were somewhat surprised to see Gina there, gazing at her with tender interest, and seemed to sense a potential conquest.

Czołhański, representing his paper and seated in the first row, also noticed us. "Where is Mr. Witold?" he asked, scanning the hall. "I've been waiting for him, but he hasn't arrived."

"Unfortunately," I replied in a rather dry tone, "I'm not in a position to enlighten you. However, if he has made an appointment with you, you can expect him to show up."

In reality, though, I was quite sure that Witold would be absent. He had even advised me not to attend the concert, as he particularly wanted me to be at home with him. Still, I didn't want to disappoint Gina.

"He promised to be here for sure," Czołhański repeated as he walked away.

I soon noticed Owiński strolling up the central aisle alongside a lady in black attire, no longer young. He held some tickets and, despite his shortsightedness, tried to find the corresponding numbers of the chairs. A pretty girl accompanied the lady in black; her dark eyes sparkled, and she seemed quite impressed by the importance of the performance. She spoke in a low tone to her fiancé, playfully teasing him about his embarrassment, and then found their seats not far from us, on the opposite side of the central aisle.

Owiński excused himself from the company of the ladies and was in the midst of searching for something when he happened to spot us as he walked by.

His complexion changed subtly, and he then approached to pay his respects, gently kissing Gina's hand without uttering a word. Similarly, she remained silent, not lifting her eyes.

I commended him for securing the talented performer Ileska to recite his poem. He responded with a few courteous words and departed. A brief silence ensued.

A tall young musician, his fingers elegantly tapering, released a cascade of harmonious notes that evolved into increasingly enchanting melodies. The music alternated between delicately rounded pearls and harsh, angular tones, echoing thunder and hail. A mournful wail emerged, Gina bowed her head, and then the dawn triumphantly arrived amidst pealing bells. The artist in refined evening attire continued, his hands falling gently on the piano keys like velvet, occasionally producing a rapid, unseen gesture that scattered a shower of musical pearls from his inexhaustible repertoire.

I've never been able to be captivated by music at any concert. I listen, I watch, and I might even be impressed. However, to be truly captivated requires seclusion and concentration. There are moments when I prefer a barrel organ to a concert!

I coolly admired the impressive technique of the young virtuoso, making his public debut, and the captivating charm that seemed almost like hypnotism or magic. Gina sat spellbound, closely watching every movement of his hands. She no longer glanced towards her triumphant rival, but a shadow passed over her face, and she furrowed her golden brows, displaying a deep frown.

I turned my gaze towards Owiński, but our eyes met with two black, observant ones. Ah, she was scrutinizing Gina!

Silence fell, followed by applause as the actress, thin and unassuming, stepped onto the platform. She offered a formal nod, surveying the hall with a serious expression. The audience waited, filled with anticipation and excitement.

A crisp, clear, and cold voice resonated through the brilliantly illuminated hall. Gradually, as if setting the stage for a surprise, it transformed into a mysterious, soft, and low timbre. The imagery evoked marble terraces leading to subterranean vaults. The words took on sculpted forms through her articulate delivery, the tones descending into the mutterings of a hushed lament, the barely audible murmurs of a curse, and the profound depths of the agony of death.

At intervals, Ileska would pause, casting her eyes down. In an ecstatic concentration of self-suggested rapture, she waited while her remarkable voice echoed off the white and lofty walls, filling her attentive ears. She would then open her large, somber eyes, continuing the recitation, seemingly inspired by the sound of her own unique voice.

Indeed, she infused the poem she admirably recited with so much of her distinctive individuality that, at first, I failed to recognize it as Owiński's work. Gina, writhing with anguish, raised her eyes, tilting her head back, staring into the electric candelabra's glare. She blinked occasionally, attempting to push back a couple of tears that sparkled in each outer corner of her eyes, trying to contain them within her heart. Ah, yes, I know that trick well. But it was unsuccessful; indeed, it does fail from time to time. Two translucent pearls slowly trickled onto her temples, lost in the tresses of her brown hair.

Following Ileska, Miss Iseult Lermeaux, a singer predicted by Czołhański to be the concert's main attraction, stepped onto the platform. Her figure, upon seeing it, struck me as strangely familiar. Could it be? No, the notion seemed incredible. I furrowed my brows to concentrate my attention to be sure. No, only a fearful, unaccountable pain had momentarily seized me. It was Gina's pain that I felt, reflected within myself—an inexplicable enchantment, perhaps rooted in the drawn-out, lazy, lascivious, dreamy notes of the Southern land song she sang. Yes, it may be that.

No. No. NO.—It is she, none but she... she beyond all doubt. Now I know, and my knowledge is hell to me. Yes, I know all.

Ah! She is beautiful, divinely so! The combined power of the senses and the refined nuances of art have collaborated to craft an irresistible allure that she effortlessly radiates. No, not a word! Those eyes, astonishing in their fairy-like beauty, and the long lashes that fringe them—those drowsy yet unfathomable eyes, reminiscent of her whom King Cophetua cherished so dearly! Yes, and her mouth, too—that wondrous, wondrous mouth, now pale and wan from excess delights, either felt or known only in dreams. But, Heavens! I can see this mouth pressed close to that other mouth, sweet beyond all sweetness—that mouth redolent with its dangerously intoxicating scent, a scent akin to withered roses!

This—this is not death!

Not at all. Oh no, it is not death: this is Life! Understand the truth. It is life; witness it now: life in its truest form.

Do you see now? All is clear. Czołhański awaited him here for that reason. He wished for you not to come, and because you came, he stayed away.

Is—isn't this still Death?

No. It is Life: Life that, from the supremely melodious, drowsy, sleepy yet fiery voice emanates; from the languid, lascivious curves of her limbs; from those shapely, slender glossy shoulders and outstretched naked arms, resembling pale dead gold, has surged forth toward you with all its formidable might!

Gina, lost in dreary amazement, stared at me.

"What ails you? Should we not leave this place?"

Both of us soon found ourselves, frantic with pain, in the brightly lit street, illuminated by the flaring windows of the grand hall, as bright as day.

"Let's go away—far away! Home? Absolutely not. Get drunk somewhere—lose my senses—spill someone's blood."

I was ranting like one in delirium.

"I beg you, Gina, come, come along—I can't bear any more!" I stammered.

She hesitated. "Unaccompanied and alone—to an all-night bistro?"

"What does it matter?"

"Perhaps we should have made an appointment—with Mr. Imszański."

Then I burst into laughter. "Unaccompanied? Ha, ha, ha!" I bellowed as we stepped into a coach. "Forgive me, but even so, I don't think either of us has much to lose!

"To the Lipka? I won't. No, I implore you. No reminiscences of the past—A café, any café! Or a top-notch bistro. Quick! As fast as the horses can go! Faster, faster!"

The great black half-starved horses took off. A few street lamps flickered by in the dark night. A few jolts from the rubber-tired wheels made us sway about: and again, everything is bright around. Oh! How I am tormented!

A cold gust blows, muddy puddles splash, a drizzling rain begins. Oh, yes, yes; all this is very real: fact, not fiction.

Now, a brilliantly lit entrance is before us; now, a staircase adorned with flowers and mirrors.

Gina stared at me in astonishment, but she uttered not a single word. She must have been unable to fathom what had come over me. However, in her state of mind, the strangest occurrence must have seemed quite ordinary. And then, she no longer felt so alone in her distress; compared to my madness, her tearful dejection seemed insignificant.

The grand hall was, as usual, filled with representatives of the jeunesse dorée,[26] financiers, and courtesans. We attracted quite a bit of attention. I had adopted the cheerful demeanor of a girl ardently seeking amusement, looking around lively at everyone. Several men approached me.

In the passage leading to the doors of the private supper-rooms, we encountered a young but mature satyr who linked his arm with mine and peered into my face. Yet, I did not stop laughing. Revenge was what I sought—debauchery—oblivion of all!

Gina's terrified gaze implored me.

"We have nothing to lose," I responded to their silent plea. And then she, too, began to laugh in a peculiar manner.

The creature whose arm linked with mine kept talking incessantly... about I don't know what. A waiter courteously opened the door to a small private room, and the three of us entered.

"I presume, ladies, you've been at the play?" our companion inquired, observing our attire.

"Ha, ha!" I replied. "Spot on. Seen one play, here for another." My tones were as coarse and ribald as my words.

"That's excellent. Waiter, the menu! What will you have?"

"To eat, nothing. We want to drink, drink, drink!"

"Very well!" he exclaimed, pleasantly surprised. "Coffee and liqueur—cognac—champagne?"

"Sure thing: anything and everything, my dear man!"

Several bottles adorned the table. Our companion, leisurely preparing a sauce, relished the lobster, displaying his white teeth in a grin. Gina sipped her drink but remained silent. I prattled incessantly, attempting to pass myself off as a coquette. Despite this, we remained an enigma to the young man, and his behavior lacked assurance.

"Do you know, Madame," he finally blurted out, addressing me, "it would be more enjoyable if we made it a quartet. I have an acquaintance in the salon here: a great fellow."

Then, turning to Gina: "You too, Madame," he said, "should have a little diversion."

I strongly objected.

"No need for him; let him stay put. You're what we're after."

I restrained him, placing my hands on his shoulders, and my face close to the unknown man's animalistic visage.

He smiled, quite flattered; his white teeth gleamed.

"We won't keep you long if you want to leave. But for now, you have to stay."

Someone—perhaps the waiter—filled my liqueur glass with cognac repeatedly. Soon, a crimson, blood-red smoke wafted through the small, red-and-gold-papered room, filled with loud voices and tobacco fumes. Everything around me seemed ablaze.

He approached; I felt his presence in every fiber of my being. His jaws, still chewing though supper was over; his small eyes, glowing phosphorescent with anticipation; the hot, foul breath from his open mouth, adorned with shining fangs and incisors; and that blond, erect mustache—I had all these close to my face. Unsteadily leaning in, he tilted his chair towards the sofa, touching and fingering the gauze trim of my bodice, seeking my lips.

My brain, intensely stimulated, presented reality. Yet, I half-closed my eyes, looking at him through the lids as if on the verge of fainting.

All efforts were in vain. My mind regained sobriety, and its faculties came into full operation.

In that moment, I recoiled and, fueled by the intensity of my rage, hatred, despair, and the thirst for revenge—for everything and everyone—I delivered a fierce blow with my clenched fist right between those lustful, phosphorescent greenish eyes!

He staggered and tumbled, along with his chair, onto the floor. Gina swiftly reached the door.

I slammed all the money I had onto the table and, shutting the door behind us, hastily left with Gina.

The passage was empty. I exited the salon, my face now wearing an indifferent expression. In the cloakroom, we donned the hooded mantles we had brought to the concert. I returned home, utterly drained of strength and in a state of complete collapse.

Gina, an extraordinary woman, never asked for any explanation.

"This explosive scene has done me good," was her indifferent and only remark.

From that day forth, I became her friend.

I recounted the entire ordeal to Gina, from start to finish. She considered me terribly naïve. "Things could not have turned out differently," she said. She advised me to forgive Witold. Only if he had loved another could I have a legitimate grievance. But a passing connection like that! Furthermore, I had no claim over him; and besides, he was a man! Owiński, too, had been unfaithful to her several times, and though their circumstances were different from ours, she had always pardoned him—albeit not without difficulty. It was only now that she truly grasped the depth of suffering. If he had been willing, she would have allowed him a dozen affairs alongside his marriage!

"Never would I agree to such a thing," I retorted. "If Witold abandoned me for the love of another woman, at least I'd be certain that my misery served a purpose for others. Both sides would have equal rights, as I could just as easily have fallen for someone else. But if he's unfaithful for a mere dalliance, amusing himself with what means no more to him than a good cigar, then I'm absolutely powerless and defenseless against him. I could never, ever reciprocate. The immense disproportion between his transgression and my retribution makes me absurd in my own eyes. When Rosławski left me, I was also devastated, but his actions were never as mean and dirty as this."

"I have no desire," responded Gina, "to impose my life philosophy on you."

He has apologized, even sworn that I am mistaken. I refused to believe him. Women are incredibly trusting, exceedingly so.

I haven't seen him all week. He came by twice, but I denied him entry. I'm not a fan of the forgiving system. I don't want to become like Marta.

However, in reality, I am tormented by his absence. My emotions lead me to believe that he might be telling the truth. Surely, he cannot be this false to me.

I fear greatly that if he comes again…

No, no. I'm going to visit Wiążewski, who has been quite neglectful lately.

I started by complaining about things in general, with little personal feeling. He has known nothing about my relationship with Witold so far. I'm also ashamed of this love, where I've played such a ludicrous part.

"And to think of the years, the golden years of youth, slipping away, beautiful, but as empty as some ancient marble bath!"

"But I told you once that men of modern times do not care to bathe in those waters. They are too clear, too cold; they flow with too swift a stream and too many, oh! far too many eddies and deep hollows. Janka, they fail to attract."

"Let me tell you, Stefan, that I am unhappy, and therefore come to you. You, as a friend, have some responsibilities toward me; you can't escape them. All that I am is falling apart at this time, and I do not know whether life or death will come of the change taking place."

I had never yearned for Witold as at that moment, even though I knew no one had wronged me as he had.

"What about Helen?" I asked, with friendly interest.

"There again! I have been disappointed in her."

"What, she! Unfaithful to you? Can that be?"

"Ah, no! I, rather than she, have been at fault in that respect."

"Well then?"

"Well, what shall I say? I have broken up with her."

Forsaken! She too had now joined the list after Marta, Gina, and myself!

"That's horrible. She was so much in love with you."

"Whereas I, alas! have a preference for women who care for nothing much."

"Yet I know you've been moody lately."

"And you are right: yes, I have."

"Well, what troubled your Olympian calm? The parting scene—tears—upbraiding?"

"Not in the least. She left without saying a word."

"Then what was it?"

"I've simply lost my belief in the last dogma left to me from childhood. Everyone complains that women lack heart, brains, and soul; and now I find that it's in vain I've sought a woman devoid of those superfluous qualities."

"But Helen, as I understood, perfectly matched your ideal of a woman?"

"I fondly thought she did. Oh, you cannot imagine what I would give to meet a woman truly soulless, primitive: you know, a creature absolutely and bewilderingly unenlightened."

"Really, I quite dislike you today, Stefan. You are positively in bad form!"

"Please forgive me."

"What specific mark of her culture did Helen give you?"

"Culture? That would have been far too bad. Besides, it was perhaps something even worse: a mark of character, firm conviction.

"Up until now," he continued, "I had been quite content with the girl; so, a few days ago, I suggested that she should quit her job and come to live with me. Can you believe it? I faced a direct refusal. You might think she wanted marriage or something of that sort; and, word of honor! If she did, I would have accepted willingly. Not at all. She sagely told me that 'although she acknowledged free love, she would never be a kept woman!' What do you make of that, eh? Ha, ha! It's quite astounding, isn't it?"

But I couldn't laugh. I sat in silence, pondering many things, more troubled than amused.

Stefan continued: "A girl with such splendidly expressionless eyes of a bright azure, like a piece of water! No shadow of any yearning for the Beyond, no hint of anything resembling intellect or brightness of thought! By day, they reflected the sun, her lamp in the evening, and my own eyes at night. They had the beautiful, lifeless gleam of pearls. She might have been less pretty; with such eyes, she was pretty enough for me. And then, that slow, sleepy, brainless sensuality in her gaze! And her white flashing teeth too! I tell you, there isn't a single spot or flaw in any one of them; her molars are like the molars of a ruminant, large and flat. True, she did write me letters unnecessarily; but, under my influence and guidance, she had even come to forget her alphabet. She truly gave me the impression (though false, as I know now) that she never thought at all.

"And that girl 'acknowledges free love'! Such a revelation may well make one cast all the beliefs of one's life onto the dustheap!"

All this discourse seemed decidedly shallow and foolish to me. Why on earth was he trying, through his far-fetched theory, to justify the fact that the woman simply bored him?

He has now resolved to seek his future Dulcineas among kitchen maids.

"Dressmakers have decidedly too much culture for my taste," he said.

"I sincerely hope you may be successful," was my parting wish.

Contrary to my expectations, Witold hasn't called again. There's something going on that's beyond my understanding.

I'm bombarded by countless thoughts that make me pale with fear.

Perhaps he, too, is "seeking oblivion," as I was, but he's unlikely to stop in time like me. Besides, his vengeance won't be a more dreadful pain than the injury itself, unlike mine.

He has a supremely great advantage over me, and the conditions of the struggle are extremely unequal.

Will he delay his visit for long? Is it conceivable that he has given me up forever?

I was in tears all evening.

Idalia felt it her duty to try and comfort me. She's a kind, lovable girl who knows how to skillfully navigate through various emotional nuances. Her eyes are gentle, her face slightly faded and careworn; there's something maternal about her.

"We take everything so seriously, so much *au tragique*," she says. "And that, you see, puts us more in their power. We should analyze things less and learn to glide over them. Analysis is a two-edged weapon; it easily turns and wounds you. Do try to pass along with a cursory look about you, even with half-closed eyes; things will seem different at once. Don't cry anymore, and if he should come, the servant is to let him in, isn't she?"

"On no account; on no account," I cried, in a fury.

"But why?" she murmured, gently stroking my hair. "Why? Letting him in doesn't bind you in any way; you are free to act as you like. And why not hear what he has to say?"

"Because I have heard him already."

"And you wouldn't believe him? You were not right in that. It is so easy to believe! And whether the thing is true or not, what does it matter to you? What is true at some point in time may be false in some part of space; and vice versa. A fact is true, but only for the day. When he is beside you and assures you of his love, you will have the greatest of all truths: the indubitable truth in the present. What took place before? What is to come later? Never mind: it is all the same!"

And I think she is right.

Every now and then, Czołhański pays me a visit. He did so yesterday as well. This, I think, is rather too much. Good

Lord! how I detest that man! He walks in, takes a seat, stays for three endless hours, throws a few compliments my way, and spouts some commonplace remarks about the lamentable state of a journalist: a man untidy, unshaven, somewhat unclean in his habits, and excessively pretentious. His fingernails are in mourning, and his hands are always moist. No use picking up a newspaper, even to be more discourteous to him; he won't take the hint and leave. He once wrote a sonnet for me! Journalism has evidently killed his poetic talent. But, goodness! what does it all matter in the end? He insists on kissing my hands, despite my constant pleas for him not to, as he disgusts me. If I were in his place, I would go and hang myself! Yet, he remains blissfully unaware of my feelings, quite self-satisfied.

Yesterday, Radłowski also came, claiming to bring a message from Gina. His company would be most pleasant as he is exceedingly young, and his eyes sparkle like a diamond in the sun, with a kind of delight so vivid that it seems unnatural; painfully so. He has once again asked me to sit for my portrait. I have promised, but I cannot—I cannot as yet.

Why is Idalia playing so poorly today? She twists and turns at the piano with more than sensual affectation; she suddenly and convulsively coils and uncoils herself like a snake during the more brilliant passages. She continues playing endlessly, from dusk until far into the deep, dark, never-ending night.

And why is she doing so on this particular day, when all my strength to bear it has left me? The longing, the pain I feel, is stifling, strangling me; it bites at my throat, and I shudder as it clings around my feet like ivy, together with the thought of my blighted joys. I see them lying on heaps of tropical flowers—lying in long rows, naked, asleep, and beautiful as dreams of what is past forever. Over them blows a gentle breeze, scattering the flower petals upon their fairy-like forms; it does not wake them from slumber. Only, from time to time, do their long black eyelashes open and shut, slowly and rhythmically, like the silken wings of a fluttering butterfly. They are dreaming of their delights.

Say, oh say! Why does all of this inflict upon me such boundless pain?

Then, there come to me persistent visions, echoes of my childhood! A dark silhouette of forest trees; a perspective fading into infinite, infinite distance, and the clear waters where life once lay hidden. The vision stands, I know not how, for the times of my childhood. Music always renders concrete even the most abstract of things.

Something is tearing at my soul; it is the impossibility of any delusion about... Oh, do not, do not bite thus at my throat! I cannot weep! And do not make the sharp-edged music of the violin soft by the dark velvet touch of your smooth hand! And do not, do not press my bosom so; my heart will burst! And do not hug my body with that tender embrace, that sensual caress! Nor twine like ivy around my feet, uttering that awful moan for blighted joys! Witold, O Witold! Behold, I return to you! O sleep, O life! Yes, I return.

Today, I have penned the following brief note to Witold:

"If you wish, you may come. J. D."

It exuded the spite—the unavailing and very plebeian spite—of my humiliation. I fully recognized this, and yet I chose to send the note in this manner.

I expected him to come like a conqueror, triumphant and self-assured; thinking so, I, for the time being, ceased to love him at all.

As it happened, he defied my expectations. Upon my return from the office, I found him already here. He was quite childishly delighted, and for a long while, I could not free myself from his rapturous embrace.

"Janka, Janka! How cruel, how cruel you have been!" he cried out in broken words among his kisses. "You are a monster of barbarity! And of stubbornness too! For you know so well how much I love you! You should have had trust in me, as I have trust in you. Have I ever given you any cause for mistrust? I hide nothing from you, nothing whatsoever! Oh, my dearest, my only one, my darling! I know that you will be mine one day—mine! It must be so. Could I ever have exposed myself to the danger of losing your love? Think of that. Think how different you are from all other women. I know you could never have forgiven me if..."

So handsome, so kindly, so affectionate! I knew how intensely I loved him. And then, in the secret depths of my heart of hearts, I was aware that I could forgive him anything in the world.

Yet I said: "My love for you would then instantly turn to hate, as it did for the last few days."

He pretended to be horribly frightened. We were both of us in ecstasies of joy.

We spoke at length about our love. We pledged to love each other eternally and with unparalleled intensity. The commitment was to be fortified by increased mutual trust and a higher level of tolerance, leaving behind the previous discord that had been so painful for both of us.

As we drew closer, I felt almost delirious with ecstasy. The air around me took on a rosy hue, the walls seemed to emit a purple glow, and the lamp burned with an indescribable intensity—black, entirely black! Lowering his head, he fixed his eyes on me.

"Janka!" he uttered with subdued yet distinct articulation. His voice had changed, carrying a restrained and fervent emotion. There was a hint of surprise in it, anticipation of the victory he foresaw.

Startled, a shiver ran through me. A tumultuous noise echoed in my ears like a whirlwind, my throat filled with a hot, suffocating fragrance, and the air I breathed felt solid and came in fragments.

"Janka, Janka," he whispered again, grappling with his profound agitation. In a hypnotic trance, I gazed into his dimly glistening eyes. I kissed his mouth, and in that kiss, my entire soul, with all its faculties, was concentrated and poured out!

I cannot fathom what held me back at that moment, as everything I possessed had transformed and converged into a single desire. No longer thirst but hunger—fierce, ravenous hunger. I clung to him desperately, stammering a string of broken, incoherent words. In a delirium of mixed agony and bliss, I sighed under my breath:

"Oh, my only one; oh, my own!"

Afterward, when he left unfulfilled and disappointed, as usual, I collapsed on the floor near the closed door. With heart-rending tears, I listened to the fading sound of his footsteps and implored:

"Oh, come—come—come back! I am yours!"

Yet, even if he had returned, I knew I would resist, as I always do. Perhaps such a thirst as mine cannot be quenched by any earthly delight!

Everything is back to its former state. I find myself deeply in love, somewhat content, and adopting a slightly sarcastic stance towards life in general. Witold visits me daily, displaying kindness and tenderness beyond words.

At times, our conversations lose momentum. In those moments, we turn to reading together—only novels and poems, as scientific literature is non-existent in Witold's world. A recently published volume of Owiński's poems has provided us with many pleasant hours.

Idalia is correct: I took everything, including matters of the heart, too seriously. I am trying to live more practically than ever before.

The current situation offers no prospects for marriage or any significant development. As I see it, it might last at most one more year. I need to be prepared for that inevitability, allowing the separation to occur gradually and as smoothly as possible. Occasionally, when I reflect on the ideals I once cherished, the notion of a love both deep and wise still crosses my mind, albeit rarely.

Perhaps it would be wiser to seek something beyond love—an "aim in life," an idea, asceticism, or even the sanctuary of a nunnery. "*Dans la bête assouvie un ange se réveille*!" Yes, but is it truly "*assouvie*"?[27] Well, I am rather fatigued, not only by love but by the entire atmosphere in which I dwell.

In reality, disdain for all things seems the best option. Yet, once again, disdain itself becomes one of the things to be disdained!

I am presently entangled in a curious situation, and I can barely recognize myself as that "She of the Plains of ice." In this continuous struggle with myself, my strength has been depleted.

Ah, yes, another incident. Czołhański has proposed to me in the most naïve manner imaginable. Despite being a woman with "advanced" ideas (and they say such a woman may not make a good wife), he remains unalarmed; he trusts in me! Additionally, he could not coexist with a woman incapable of understanding him. Also, he receives two hundred rubles a month, which, combined with my office salary… and so on.

I have categorically, hopelessly, and irrevocably declined his proposal. Strangely enough, I did so without the shadow of a smile.

When I'm utterly exhausted and feeling off, I reach out to Wiążewski. Some individuals resemble the ships once utilized by slave traders, featuring a double hold. Wiążewski is akin to such vessels.

He willingly and openly lets anyone inspect his soul upon request. However, when they come knocking on the hold, he prefers them not to be too forceful. The hollow sound beneath might expose his secret. Beneath the false bottom lies a dark chamber where he smuggles those he has ensnared, never to emerge freely into the world again.

Knowledge of this would tarnish his reputation as an upstanding individual in society.

"Do you know, Stefan, you appear like a man with a hint of tragedy on his conscience, concealing it."

He laughed. "Since when did Janka become so romantic?"

"Since I fell in love, of course!"

"You?!" Astonished, he stared at me.

"My dear friend, why should that surprise you?"

"I genuinely... no, really, I don't know. I was merely taken aback. Certainly, from your side, it's only natural. Don't you see? I had grown so accustomed to considering you as belonging to a third sex."

"There now, how unjust you've been! For my part, I've always viewed you as a man."

"But come, tell me with whom you're in love and whether your bliss is as fantastic as one might imagine."

I shrugged my shoulders.

"Bliss! It's you who are romantic now, Stefan. At best, I'm not bored. And the less bliss I have, the less bored I am!"

"Then you're not bored?"

"Oh, I am—very much so at times. In those moments, I come and visit you. I've learned to cherish our disinterested friendship more and more."

He shifted, slightly annoyed, then lit a cigarette.

"Whom?"

"I don't understand."

"Whom do you love?"

"Oh, an ideal according to your own taste. *A bon entendeur salut.*"[28] (Note: All the better if you've caught my meaning.)

"Won't you tell me?"

"No, I won't. Guess, if you want to know."

"A fool?"

"To some extent, yes."

"Handsome?"

"Too much by far."

"Wealthy?"

"Indifferently."

"It is—it is Imszański! *Et tu*, Janka!" he exclaimed, looking into my face with a curious expression.

I knew what question was implied by his look and slowly shook my head.

He breathed more freely.

"And yet I would never have imagined."

"How's that? I have only been practicing your own theory of love."

"Ye—es, but...."

"Well, but what?"

"This is quite another thing. Of primitive elemental simplicity, he has nothing at all."

"It is true. In that point, and in that point only, has my practice departed from your theory. But I think good art is not unfrequently preferable to problematical simplicity."

"Yes, no doubt. And, moreover...."

"Pray continue."

"I myself have ended by abandoning that theory of mine. My experience with Helena exploded it definitely. I have radically changed my attitude; now I am without any conviction at all on the subject."

"But I imagined that the fallen edifice of your theory was to be restored by the aid of kitchen-maids."

"Vain hopes! They have proved impracticable, even to myself. My experiments in that quarter only completed the ruin of the theory."

"Well, then, what are you going to do about it?"

"I am seeking love."

"Oh, dear! *Et tu!* And it was to you I came on purpose to get a rest from it. There must be some fatality about all this—the atmosphere is vitiated everywhere. Stefan, have mercy, have mercy!"

He smiled compassionately.

"So soon as that? Janka, how soon you get tired!"

We went to a café, where we saw Gina sitting along with Radłowski at one of the tables. There were none vacant, so we joined them at theirs, and I introduced the men to each other. Wiążewski objects to artists; but he must have been pleased with this one, whose exterior is that of a typical "gentleman." I was in exceedingly good spirits, and set about flirting with the painter. He was now much changed from what he was when I saw him last. His eyes are not bright anymore, and he looks a good deal older. We fell to talking upon speculative subjects, and I strove to be original and sparkling. Radłowski's eyes were fixed steadfastly on my face all the while.

"Well, I see you are far more of a woman than I had ever thought you."

My response to Stefan's words was just a glance, but a glance of triumph. Finally, this, the most challenging victory of all, had arrived! Unfortunately, it came too late.

"In a few years," he added, "when all your faculties are properly balanced, you will be an exceptional being. Perhaps a model 'Woman of the Future.'"

"Oh, anything but that. I take no interest except in what goes on within me. If I am at all elated, it is not on account of what is there, but of the fact that these forces are incessantly in conflict with my will. I am proud of my imperfections, which turn to perfections, of my ideas that treat one another with mutual contempt, of my instincts so strongly opposed to my logic; of my archaic tendencies, which it is a finer and more momentous work to unearth and to note down than to put into practice. I am proud of the eternal Becoming, teeming with riches, dazzling with the wildest hues, deafening with harsh discordances, rushing on, stirring all about, turning in spiral ascension, or even spinning around. Yes, I am proud that this Becoming still goes on. I prefer a hundred times the 'Transitional Woman' to the 'Woman of the Future': because she who is transitional has so much more promise than the other, when perfect, can fulfill.

"Neither you," I said, turning to Gina, "with your quasi-Pantheistic theory of love; nor Madame Wildenhoff, with her volatile and almost man-like eroticism; nor Idalia, nor

Marta—none of you is, any more than I am, a woman of the future; you are full of exaggerated theories, of oddities, of false notions, of archaic trends, and extreme views. Yet I prefer you to that free and happy woman of our dreams, in whom desire, conscious and in perfect equilibrium, will not, however intense it may be, trespass beyond the limits of its possibility to be satisfied. Yes! You I prefer to the most perfect of standards, to the very best of patterns, to the wisest and most consistent of Philistines!"

Gina said gloomily:

"Then what is it all for—this ghastly struggle, this agony of Becoming?"

"For the glory of the last specimens of our species. We are tending towards this goal: that the abstract type of Woman may perish as soon as it is realized, just as the abstract type of Man also perishes. Having attained that level, we shall, together with Man, begin to evolve in the wider sphere of our common humanity. The struggle and the war of the elements which make up our nature will still continue in a new Becoming, but no longer in the narrow space of womanhood, which leaves us too little room to breathe."

"All the same," said Stefan, in conclusion, "our descendants will envy us very, very much, since we live in the days of the Last Woman."

"Let's hope that the present period may endure for some time; say, until the gorilla is extinct."

Stefan's feeling of medieval worship for woman was shocked at my words: "Women and gorillas named together!" he sighed.

While we were going home, after taking leave of Gina and Radłowski, he said, hesitatingly and in some confusion:

"Janka, do not make a pastime of that Imszański any more: he is not worth playing with."

"Well said, but?..."

"Hear me out, Janka. Till the present moment, I was not aware that I loved you and you alone. May I hope, or is it quite out of the question?"

"Good God, Stefan! pray don't think of proposing! I got a proposal only the other day. There must be something in the air—infection—the approach of spring! At any rate, I am not in a consenting mood now; so, let me be."

I laughed, but was in reality very much upset.

When last together, Gina asked me to come over to her apartments, as she wanted me to read something she had.

It was almost gayly that she welcomed me in. Her eyes had lost their customary look of apathy, and shone with a strange fire.

"Owiński is going to be married this very week," she remarked, as if stating a fact which did not concern her. "Have you read his poems?"

"I have; Witold and I read them together."

"One of his poems had been dedicated to me; I know, for I myself saw it in a proof—a proof that I myself corrected. And now the dedication has been removed from the title. When he received the revised proof, he probably crossed it off."

She then took two closely written sheets of letter-paper out of a drawer.

"A letter from her!" she explained.

"To you?!"

"Yes. Just read it."

It ran thus:

"I have long been wishing to write to you, Madame; and if I have not made up my mind till now, this was neither from any want of courage on my part, nor any misplaced sense of delicacy, which would in this case be not only exaggerated, but groundless. It simply proceeded from the fact that, as I think the greatest alleviation of sorrow consists in the possibility of hating someone on account of it, I did not want to deprive you of the object of your hate.

For I am of opinion that, as soon as you have read this, you will not think of me as your enemy any more.

"If I write now, it is because I believe that, in lieu of such consolation, I am able to afford you another; and I do so without the knowledge of my fiancé, for I have my doubts whether it would be pleasant to him or the reverse; and besides, I do not consider him as the sole means by which we might come to understand each other.

"The evening on which we were both under the same roof has remained with me as a painful memory. Not because I blamed on your account. As I had been aware from the beginning that O. was affianced, I played no active part in the matter to attract him. Any other woman might have been in my place, and done just the same, so far as you were concerned. O. was at that time in want of a figure upon his life chessboard, such as is called a formally affianced wife; so, we met and encountered each other by mere chance—a happening without logical relevance to anything. Nor was it because I felt pity for you. My mind would never consent to abase you by venturing to entertain such a feeling; and I think, too, that I am an object of pity no less than yourself. No; the meeting was painful to me only for the following reason; I myself, looking on things as an outsider, cannot help having a fellow-feeling for all who have been defeated; so that I experienced self-dislike. It was painful, because I was present in your mind as a stranger, a successful rival, nothing but the fiancée of your fiancé, a hostile, unknown She: not a woman, drawn close to you by your and my sense of our hard fate. It was painful for me to sit so far apart from you, to be unable to approach you and look into your thoughtful eyes with eyes that were no less thoughtful, and kindly too, and talk to you about many subjects far more important than the law which thrusts us apart: the law, known from time immemorial, that love is not everlasting, and that it needs variety.

"To write of my friendly feeling towards you would certainly seem somewhat paradoxical. I will therefore say no more than this; I deeply and sincerely esteem you, as one after my own heart, as a New Woman, a woman conscious of her own value and of her rights; I appreciate you also for your subtlety of emotion, and your original artistic talent. And then, besides, I have a certain debt of gratitude which is due to you personally, and owing to the fact that O. has for several years been faithful to you; and thus, the list of his transitory amours which distress me so is considerably shorter than it would otherwise have been. I bear you no grudge, no, not even when O. (for my enjoyment!) goes back into the past, and tells me all about his former love for you.

"I trust you no longer feel any instinctive dislike or aversion for me; do you? And now I will, in return for what you have to suffer, give you the information that you have indeed but very little reason to envy my lot. Like you, I am one of those unhappy beings who must suffer, whatever their circumstances may be, because life is too brutally inexorable, and we—we whose nerves are laid bare—cannot walk through life without suffering. Then, examining the question quite objectively, may we not unhesitatingly assert that it is preferable to endure suffering for a positive loss, whilst we enjoy the memory of past happiness (or at least the illusion that such happiness would have been possible, had circumstances and environment been different), rather than to endure it at that one period of our lives when we ought not to suffer at all? than to experience such distress as excludes the possibility that we may so much as dream of ever being happy? Is misery not at its height in the very springtime of life when the faculty of possible enjoyment is most developed? In this indeed, the lot of our fiancé is always and invariably an enviable one. I am not happy, and I doubt whether you have ever known happiness. A strange being he is, forever plucking flowers and smiling in the sunshine, yet unceasingly, and often unwittingly, marking his road through life by the pain he gives to others, and by the tears, so vain and so unworthy of us, which he makes us shed.

"So, I am not writing to you in order that I may enjoy my honeymoon without remorse, for—as I say once more—I do not consider that I have done you any wrong. I only want you to know me just as I am, and not look upon me as a stranger or an enemy. I am not given to sentiment, and do not fear the hatred of people: on the contrary, I rather like it; but I do not wish you to hate me. What a sad thing it would be, if a poet could succeed in separating two intelligent and agreeable women from each other forever!

"I kiss you, and with the warmest affection."

"A sweet creature she is!" I remarked, and looked at Gina.

She was looking depressed, and much older. Her eyes were bedimmed, and wandering helplessly from piece to piece of furniture, from wall to wall.

"And she does not even feel any love for him! A cold-hearted being, made for nothing but to chop logic! And he—for her, for her! Oh, the cruel wrong! Why has this come to me?"

She put her hands up to her head and sobbed aloud.

Suddenly she snatched the letter from me, and crumpled it up, and tore it all to pieces with angry fingers.

"How I hate, oh, how I hate that woman!"

I brought her a glass of water to calm her nerves, and I thought how much more preferable she was—in this, her unjust outburst of fury—to the other, magnanimous, serene, lofty-minded New Woman.

Śmiłowicz, of all men in the world! was awaiting me outside the office today.

Time, I thought, had for an instant run backward; and the Past, so terribly gone and forgotten, was before me.

"What! You?!" I exclaimed; "you, back from Siberia? How long have you been here? I had not been told…"

"The manifesto: an amnesty.... Five years. Yes, five have passed by.[29] I arrived last week, and have seen nobody but

Obojański. He did not even know your address! Was that nice of you? Oh, how greatly you have changed! No, I did not expect such backsliding on your part. I have heard many things said."

"And what about yourself?"

I saw that his plain face, which was now adorned with a thin stubbly beard, was much emaciated. His former careless smile was now quite gone, and his features were darkened and bronzed like a peasant's.

"I?" He smiled, but with his lips only, that were always drawn: once with suffering, now with having suffered. "I? You never would guess. I married down there; yes, I married a fellow-exile. And we have a son."

"But what of your health? And what are you going to do in Warsaw?"

"Something or other." He raised his hand, palm down, then let it drop limply. "At present I am more or less amongst the unemployed. Besides, I now have consumption.[30] On the whole, prospects not very brilliant."

I asked him to come to my lodgings.

He looked uneasy. "Are you living with—them?" he asked.

"No; now no longer."

"Ah, that's very good. Professor Obojański told me fearful things about you, and they grieved me. He must have been exaggerating: he bears you a deep grudge for having broken up with him so. For he appreciates you very highly indeed. He counts your having thrown yourself away like that as the greatest disappointment he ever had in his life."

So, we went down the road, chatting about old times. He informed me that Rosławski had gone off on some Polar expedition. I used to call him the "Autocrat of the Plains of Ice": it seems that he belongs to them at any rate.

"But now," Śmiłowicz blurted out, rather bashfully, "hadn't you better come and see us? I have told Sofia (my wife) all about you; she would like to make your acquaintance, and does not know anybody in Warsaw. And you will see Jędruś, my little boy!"[31]

I, of course, agreed.

Madame Śmiłowicz received us in a tiny room—bachelor's lodgings on the fourth floor—amongst a confused medley of boxes and mattresses and lumber of various kinds. She began by asking us to speak low, not to disturb Andrzej, who was then asleep: then she showed him to me: a one-year-old baby, asleep in a cradle.

I paid him several compliments, of the What-a-fine-baby sort, and had not the least fear of being suspected of irony.

For the rest, Madame Śmiłowicz has not the appearance of a "youthful mother"; she is a thin, tawny little woman in a dark gown, with a double eyeglass on her nose.

She poured some spirits of wine into the little pan for heating the kettle, and while it was burning itself out, she said, very low:

"My dear Madame, people say that women are weaker than men. But they do not in the least take into account all the strength that we expend over the children; just as if it were uselessly wasted! But furthermore, and setting this aside, let any one of them try to go through what I have undergone. With a one-year-old, my dear Madame! in that bleak ice-bound land! and then, on our way home, having to do everything, my husband in wretched health. And here again, look you! notwithstanding all this work on my hands, I have managed to do quite a bit of translation: and now we shall be able to sell it somewhere. Józef dear, have you been able to see the publisher today?"

She pointed to a heap of papers, written in a fine female hand. Her husband smiled at me proudly.

As soon as the spirits were burnt out, Madame Śmiłowicz worked the piston with swift strokes, pumping up a stream of gas, while her husband held a match to light it as it issued forth. A loud droning sound was heard, and a slight smell of kerosene was discernible.

"Will the noise disturb little Jędruś?" I inquired, feigning concern.

"No, no, he's used to it by now."

We had tea, engaging in conversations about abstract topics. I hadn't read any of the books they mentioned, admitting it proved challenging. It felt like I had been transported to another planet, constantly feeling out of place and like an intruder. Moreover, my new dress starkly clashed with the surroundings, and I couldn't ignore the stark contrast with my life.

After the machine was turned off, and the noise ceased, children's voices could be heard beyond the partition wall—a commotion of many voices occasionally interrupted by a high-pitched female voice. On the fourth floor, a group of youngsters was having a lively time.

"Do you hear that, Madame? It's almost every day. They disturb my work terribly. Why are the walls so thin?"

I was astonished and couldn't help feeling somewhat envious. The contrast between us was glaring, yet she seemed oblivious to it, solely focusing on the annoyance. She made no comparisons and drew no parallels whatsoever.

Andrzej in his cradle began crying loudly.

She hurriedly got up from the table, bumping into me, and rocked the child back to sleep while singing a tuneless, wordless lullaby, reminiscent of the broken croaking of frogs. She repeatedly murmured,

"My little son, my only one, my beautiful one!"

Resuming our tea, she discussed a recently translated book—English essays on Economics. "Joseph encourages me to write something as well, but for that, one must have a more peaceful mind."

Then, casting a tender glance at her husband, she remarked, "I believe Joseph will improve in our climate. When he was sent away from Poland, he was perfectly healthy. Do you remember how he looked in those days?"

"Certainly, very well indeed."

I proceeded to reminisce about the expeditions we used to make to Obojański's.

"But," I added, "you've worked a miracle; he was always indifferent to the charms of women." I said this with kindness, fearing it might trigger jealousy or suspicion.

However, it became evident that such subtleties were lost on her; she remained impervious to any thoughts of that nature.

"When I was at the University," she shared with me, "I dedicated myself to reconciling my societal duties with those owed to my own growth. Opponents of women's emancipation argue that a woman cannot simultaneously pursue education and be a good wife and mother. It's their strongest point. But, if only women acknowledged that it's achievable, that everything can harmonize! Personally, dear Madame, I completed my Sociology course in Brussels, where I even published a short paper in French. Since then, I've kept abreast of scientific advancements to stay up-to-date. I read consistently and am currently occupied with translation. Sometimes, I assist Joseph with facts and information. Now, I ask you, dear Madame, could the most conventional bourgeois woman, placed in my circumstances, devote herself more to her child than I do? Consider, I have no nursemaid or any of the conveniences that those praised 'good mothers' enjoy. I breastfeed the baby, tidy the room, handle the cooking, and the porter delivers provisions from the market. That's all. Oh, how I wish some of those astute gentlemen could come here and see!"

"Yes," Śmiłowicz interjected, "if a working woman spends the entire day outdoors, leaving her children unattended, that's considered acceptable and reasonable! But let a woman dedicate a few evening hours to her studies, and they'll claim it's emancipation, incompatible with her duties as a mother."

I could sense her gratification upon hearing this.

"I feel sorry only for those who are unaware of the profound joy that can be discovered in marriage when there is mutual understanding and sympathy." She glanced tenderly at her husband.

Meanwhile, there was a continuous noise on the other side of the partition, accompanied by a strangely unsettling sound of women's voices, a mix of scandalized laughter—something between giggling and sobbing.

Śmiłowicz's attention was diverted by it.

"What unpleasant individuals they are!" he exclaimed finally, to vent his feelings.

"They are not malicious but unhappy," she said. "I feel sorry for them too."

Śmiłowicz remained silent. Soon, he was trying to persuade me to visit Obojański one of these days.

"Always immersed in those books of his—completely absorbed in them—indifferent to everything else happening in the wide world. His study seems to me like a haven one might dream of. Yes, let's go one day and visit him, Miss Janina."

Actually, not a bad idea. Śmiłowicz's surroundings don't agree with me. Since I've distanced myself from such associations, I have no desire to return to them. And that woman! I would gladly toss her out of the window to the Idealistic dreamer of the noble New Woman, equal to Man; and I would cry "*Ecce femina*!"[32] Like Diogenes throwing the plucked cock to Plato.[33]

Yes; for the vision of the Idealist is realized—this way!

But Obojański, the venerable, grey-bearded Master, with his demeanor of a Greek sage; and his never-ending, shallow sophistries and cheap disputes on matters of the highest import; and even his many volumes of monographs on insects—all this has something that is remarkably appealing to me!

Today, tenderness and mutual vows once more. Yes, we shall love each other until....

"Listen, Witold; how long are we to be in love like this?" I asked; a question I hadn't expected to pose.

"Forever," he answered with absolute assurance.

"And how long is this 'forever' supposed to last?"

"Ah, well—of course—as long as we live. Do you believe in love beyond the grave?"

"Decidedly not!"

"Then, until death. And as I shall surely be the first to drop off, I shall have the best of it," and he bowed like an eighteenth-century courtier in Versailles.

I focused my thoughts for a moment. Here I am, seated, adorned in the attire of ancient Greece, on a stone bench, my bare and shapely elbow resting on a balustrade. Leaning over the marble barrier, I look down, coldly, in deep analysis, into the depths beyond—the depths of my soul. And behold, it is an abyss more than of infinite depth. Alas! My reflections, depicted in this manner, only tell me that in such a posture and attire, I appear very handsome!

The sun blazes high in the sky. Drifting on the vibrant sea waves is a light boat, its prow shaped like a swan's neck, and Witold is seated in the boat. He smiles as he glides so effortlessly—sailing on the sea of life. And I—remain gazing into the depths of my own existence without purpose.

"Witold, you understand that all of this, sooner or later, must come to an end?"

"How would I know that?"

"Not from experience?"

"Ah! Janka, my dearest, how many times have I pleaded with you!" Then, in a more cheerful tone: "I am not an experimenter in any sense of the word. And that's how I know today just as much as I did yesterday, clinging to my illusions as I did in the past."

"But why won't you ever confront this question with open eyes and face it directly? Why are you always afraid of it? Why must the burden of seeing things clearly always fall on me? Oh, Witold!"

He didn't answer but paced nervously around the room. Then, stopping at a small table with his face turned away from me, he lit a cigarette.

A brief silence followed. I continued.

"It's not that I want someone to lean on. Understand me. I don't need any sustaining or protecting force. I only wish for a power capable of balancing my own. I want to be aided by strength equivalent to what I exert: I only desire an equal weight on each scale. Oh, if you only knew how terrified I am when my scale, becoming heavier, sinks down into the lowest depths of my melancholy, unfathomable pride!"

Here, I paused for a while, anticipating some response.

Out of the blue, he began to speak, calmly, in polished tones, without directing his gaze toward me.

"Let me share something with you, Janka—I've never discussed this with you before, but today I must: it burdens me too heavily, too unbearably. I might be straightforward, but I'm not a man who relishes telling the truth; I simply don't enjoy it. Well, there's one issue...."

He paused, then resumed in even smoother tones.

"There's one point—I must tell you, my dearest love, that you inflict extreme torment upon me. Yes, you do. At times, you torment me to such an extent that I lose all self-control, all patience. I am in agony, to put it plainly—I implore you, believe what I am saying now. I cannot conform myself to accept your theories. I am unable; besides, I will not. You make no sacrifice, not at all. Have you ever given up anything for my sake? No. If not, you have no right to lay down conditions. You must take me as I am; try to comprehend me and adapt yourself to me, rather than expecting me to adjust to you. Remember, I have no sympathy whatsoever with lofty sentiments; I cannot walk on stilts. I cannot, no, I cannot! All that is such a trial for me that I often yearn to escape—far away as I possibly can go! And so, I concoct untruths, invent mythical shooting and supper parties, and attend imaginary meetings—simply because I have to breathe now and then. You can see that I am currently speaking the truth! Not that I don't love you! Oh, no! If I didn't love you so deeply, so intensely—who could make me endure this even for one moment? Truly, you have no idea to what lengths of despotism your strong personality drives you. Your demands on me are endless, Janka; you confine me with your requirements and those tastes of yours that I must follow. Have I ever, in anything, interfered with you? No; I've never asserted the slightest claim to anything; in fact, I preferred you to feel, in some respect, that you were in arrears with me because I respect the liberty of others. Why can't you have the same tolerance for me? And then, for the life of me, I can't figure out why all of you are of such jealous dispositions, nor why you all persistently engage in philosophizing in that way!"

His outburst, having drained him, led him to settle into an armchair some distance away from me. He then proceeded to light another cigarette.

For several minutes, I was left speechless, attempting to navigate my way out of the wreckage of that structure that had collapsed upon me so suddenly and unexpectedly. Who would have anticipated this from my sweet page with his tawny eyelashes?

Initially, I struggled to grasp it.

"But I see, Witold, that you have no love for me whatsoever—for what is most essential in me; I've finally come to that realization."

I pondered for a moment.

"And besides, what you're saying is untrue. Remember which of us revels more in lofty, naïve, foolish, sentimental notions! Who was always dreaming of an ideal 'union of souls,' instead of viewing love in the ordinary way? It was I who cannot bear what is lofty; I, who always had to bring you down from your stilts."

Witold gazed out of the window, displaying aristocratic boredom and plain weariness in his demeanor.

"Ah, Janka," he said, this time with an air of supreme indifference, "that, too, is all theory on your part. You only use this to combat the sentimentalism within you, though you disown it and deny its existence. The eternal conflict within yourself, and your empty theories with their unconscious hypocrisy—these are the best proof of what I say, and the loftiest sentimentality of all. Only you deceive yourself. You are just like other women, capable of infinite self-devotion and sacrifice. Listen to me further. If I were to cease loving you now, leave you, and forget you (men forget so easily), you would long for me and be in anguish, like any other woman in the same situation, despite all your 'positive' theories. You would be miserable, as you were during the last two weeks when we were apart, and you would write to me first. And if I didn't respond—as I seriously contemplated not doing, despite my 'idealistic' perspective on love—then you would write again and again, even up to the tenth time! Don't say you wouldn't; I know you well. Oh, how well I know women! I'll tell you this: I am even more certain that you love me and will be faithful than I was in Marta's case, despite all you say about paying me back if I were unfaithful. Marta could forget herself for my sake; you never could. A bundle of theories, of sentimental skepticism, of self-assurance: that's what you are! A poor frightened bird always hiding its head under its wing!"

I felt utterly shattered. A vast and dreadful emptiness consumed my heart. I had a peculiar delusion—or perhaps his words induced the sensation—that I truly experienced the weakness he spoke of and was incapable of escaping from his grasp. Consequently, tears welled up in my eyes.

"I don't...I don't believe...that you ever loved me!"

Instantaneously, his demeanor shifted, returning to the kind and gentle disposition he had always displayed before. He approached my side with caresses, comforting words, and even a bit of friendly banter.

"Alas!" I groaned. "Why didn't you tell me about this before?"

"Because I was quite sure that you would burst into tears, as you're doing now, you naughty child!"

Upon hearing those words, a strong sense of distaste overcame me. A swarm of seemingly trivial incidents rushed back into my memory, along with numerous minute details from our past, serving as demonstrative and irrefutable proof of what he truly was.

"And you were quite sure, Witold, of something else as well!"

"What was that, Janka?"

With downcast eyes, I answered, smiling:

"That I would never love you again."

I spoke with absolute honesty and certainty. I knew this to be a fundamental necessity in my life, and I wiped away my last tears.

"Bah! stop it, little girl. Can't you see this is also silly sentiment? You yourself don't believe what you're saying." He continued to speak in tones of tranquil persuasion, but I could sense disquiet in his eyes.

I smiled at him once more, saying, "Whether I believe or not matters little. What matters is that you certainly do!"

He turned a shade paler and fumbled nervously for his cigarette case. "Stop it!" he suddenly exclaimed roughly, and once again moved toward me.

I stood up, quivering with excitement but managed to say, calmly enough, "I wouldn't want to part from you too dramatically. Since I've had enough of love in general, and especially of you, I'm afraid I must ask you to kindly leave now. Let's shake hands in parting. Go."

He approached with furrowed, somber brows, his gaze revealing the internal storm. I took a step back. For a moment, he wrestled with himself, and I anticipated he might charge at me.

Yet, his upbringing prevailed. He executed a refined bow, kissed my hand, and withdrew.

I stood in place, head bowed forward. That page, with his beloved tawny eyelashes—with his soft, melancholic eyes—with his lips carrying the scent of faded roses—he who had once been mine!

"Nevertheless," I whispered to myself, "the deed is finally done!"

Today, I feel like I've crossed the Rubicon and am standing on the other side, not entirely certain if things are better for me now. Still, I wouldn't wish to turn back.

This morning, I received several bouquets.

Flowers to adorn the funeral feast! Flowers on the coffin of one gone forever!

But that means nothing. No, nothing, I swear! Often, the monument over a tomb can transform into a gateway leading to a new life.

Śmiłowicz has come to visit me.

He, too, experiences mental lows at times, something I would never have suspected.

He settled into the very armchair where Witold had been seated the previous evening. He remained silent for a while, then said, "There are days when I consider myself a fool for squandering my life over a mere illusion. Oh, how I envy you!"

"Why? Is your life wasted?" I exclaimed in astonishment.

"You've been to our lodgings—and you've seen," he replied.

"Well?"

"You've seen it all!"

"But your wife seems happy," I said, attempting to take an optimistic view, though deep down, I couldn't help but wonder: "How is love possible between those two?"

"My wife might be," he said slowly. "Sometimes, I cannot."

"They say having children is a significant thing. Even if you don't achieve the goal you strive for, a part of you always remains."

My comment received no response from him. I could see painful and bitter thoughts crossing his gaunt face as he scanned the room.

"You have an abundance of flowers!" he muttered.

"These are all 'flowers of farewell.' At least, you need not envy me for these."

His face darkened.

"You know how unwell I am. That's what makes me so despicable. It's not that I regret life, but that I have nothing in life I would regret losing."

I remained silent.

"Knowing for sure that death is imminent gives you a completely different perspective on life. An extraordinary attachment to concrete things arises, along with an intense disdain for abstractions. Each renunciation, each triumph over oneself, is like a fresh nail in your coffin."

"But surely you love your wife?" I asked after a pause.

"I do."

"And your son, too?"

He nodded.

"Well, then," I tried to draw a comforting conclusion, but without success. "Well, then..." I repeated once more, lapsing into helpless silence.

"Ah, how kind you are!" he said in a low voice, gazing at me with a grateful expression. "And how beautiful, besides!" he added unexpectedly.

I felt startled, mere instinct on my part, as I had no reason to fear. He looked away from me and turned his attention to some orchids nearby, stroking them with his bony hand.

"When I ask myself now for what reason I did what I did, I can find no answer to my question. Such flowers as these; I have gone through life, always trampling upon them; why? Why should Obojański cut them to pieces, that he may, in them and from them, hit upon some new abstraction or other—their genus, their species, their variety? Why do you call them 'flowers of farewell'? Oh, now that I know how terrible the way of self-denial and virtue is, I should this day like to lie on a bed of flowers such as these."

"I can answer your question; you trampled the flowers because you were a strong man."

"Is the love of life a weakness then?" He fell into thought.

"Perhaps it is. Perhaps I care for life for the same reason that made Voltaire confess before he died: vital energy giving way. And after all, life!"

Here, I proceeded to explain to him at great length that life is, in reality, an evil and not worth regretting when it departs, leaving behind a bitterness greater than the bitterness of self-denial and self-control, and provoking a yet stronger reaction.

To that, he said, "Yes, the reaction which life brings is directed against life, and makes it easier to die. All the better."

"It is well," he added. "It is not, after all, life itself that I wish for. I wish only to be convinced—convinced by experience that life is an evil thing. This is all that I would have."

When he left me, I presented him with a great many flowers, pretending they were for his wife. Observing from the window, I saw him on his way, wearing a fur coat despite the mild weather, clutching the flowers to his heart.

In the evening, I sent a letter to Wiążewski, inviting him over. I thought he might offer some consolation, but despite his visible efforts to be in good spirits, he had none. Therefore, I suggested we take a walk.

It was a splendid night, clear and breezy, suffused with the sweet, drowsy, intoxicating scent of impending spring. The lamplights sparkled in the distance like countless strings of diamonds; the streets were deserted but brightly illuminated. The white moon occasionally peeked above the irregular line of rooftops. All was pictorially calm and cold—an atmosphere I particularly enjoyed.

Our path led us down a major thoroughfare, where a few late carriages were passing by. Stefan was telling jokes, but it felt forced. He narrated the tragic fate of a disappointed suitor.

Just ahead, at the street corner and across from a large hotel entrance, an elegantly luxurious carriage, arriving at full speed, suddenly halted. A servant rushed to open the carriage door. Witold alighted briskly, assisting a woman as she descended.

Gracefully stepping down from the carriage and walking swiftly by his side, adorned in billowing frills and lace, emanating an aura of delicate fragrances, Iseult Lermeaux entered the hotel. Witold's eyes met mine as he was about to take her arm while helping her out of the carriage. In the glow of the electric lamps, I saw him turn pale. He bowed instinctively; his arms dropped to his sides, uncertain of what to do. Wiążewski's presence seemed to embarrass him, and he stood there frozen. She also turned to glance at us.

And thus, as we walked down the long, brightly lit street, they disappeared, and we saw them no more. "No procrastination in that man!" I thought. "The very next day!"

"As I don't wish you to feel sorry for me, Stefan, I will inform you that I have already broken up with that gentleman; so his actions don't concern me at all now."

Upon my words, Wiążewski slowed his pace.

"Why, in that case, Janka…" he began.

"Please, Stefan, don't. I asked you once before—"

He remained silent then, walking for a considerable time with his head bowed down. Finally, he spoke to me in an undertone:

"Could we not consider marriage as a bond of friendship?"

"No, no! Can't you see that a wife never has the disinterestedness of a friend? How can she align herself with her husband in everything? In many cases, she would be wronging herself. For example, what interests me most in you—your disdain for things ethical and emotional—would, if I were your wife, become hateful to me. Your close understanding of feminine psychology and the art of love-making would either be perilous to me or, as a reminder of the past, unpleasant at the least. And you, you would have to become insincere; to gain a wife, you would necessarily lose a friend: and surely a friend is worth more…."

He walked along in silence, listening to me.

"And besides," I concluded, "let me tell you that you have come too late. A year ago, when you never treated me as anything but a friend, it would have been possible. Then, I was not infrequently vexed with you, calling you (I remember) a boarding school miss when you extolled friendship and poured your love theory into my ears. Today, I am not into love anymore. Not because Fate has dealt me any crushing blow. Nothing of the sort; but merely because it has all been terribly boring to me. At present, I am taking my revenge on you, in the proverbial phrase: 'Let's remain friends.'"

I quickened my pace. Wiążewski said nothing. I felt as if I were hastening towards a dark chasm that kept retreating before me as I advanced. I want it all to be over—to lie at the bottom of that murky chasm; and, no matter what I do, I cannot reach the edge. My teeth are clenched with pain.

"If you knew how madly I love the exceeding sweetness of his mouth!" The words flashed through my mind: a reminiscence of the far-off, far-off Past!

"I cannot understand you at all. Never, never, should I have acted so in your place."

"Well, Gina, it is over. Tell me now what remedy you would advise me to take. How do you yourself manage to bear life? To remain passive, doing nothing—that would surely be impossible. Work? But work is of no avail. Unless something happens to rescue me, I shall have to leave the office; I fear I am about to go mad. Are you still interested in art? You paint very little now; I cannot make out why."

Gina shook her head with a drowsy air. "I always preferred Life to Art."

"Why," I said, noticing she was in evening dress, "you are going out tonight!" The thought of staying by myself all evening made me shudder. At the same time, I felt my cheeks coloring, fearing there was a mortification in store for me that I could not understand. "I trust you will tell me quite frankly."

For a few seconds, she furrowed her brows and reflected. Then, "I think," she said, "that it will not be impossible. I have long wished to make you a proposal; but in such a matter, one cannot be too cautious. Yet, after all, we too have something in common. And I have learned to know you."

Abruptly she came to a decision.

"Then—yes, I can recommend something to you. If you hold out, it is only by its means."

"Give it to me, quick!"

"Wait a little. I must first demand that you keep this a profound secret. I hide nothing else that I do: yet this I hide. Secondly: it is something that, for effects and surroundings' sake, we do in conclave. I shall take you there."

We went.

Radłowski opened the door. When he saw me, he was taken aback, though he tried to hide it under a veneer of courtesy.

"We have a newcomer here," Gina explained.

But the explanation seemed to increase his unease rather than alleviate it, though he promptly feigned lively satisfaction. He whispered to Gina, "But something must be done: Emma is here."

Gina chuckled. "Oh, all the better! If that's your only worry!"

Radłowski was now more at ease. He ushered us into his bedroom, beyond the studio, and left us there together. Occasionally, we could hear a muffled conversation, with voices kept low, from the adjoining room.

"And who is Emma?" I inquired.

"Oh, a most beautiful woman, though not exactly welcomed in society. One of Radłowski's celebrated beauty stars, formerly a model."

Gina, picking up a small vial from the dressing table, took some of its contents herself and then instructed me on how the narcotic was to be taken.

We entered the studio, adorned with a profusion of carpets, hangings, pieces of tapestry, and low Ottomans scattered about. Nothing here betrayed the artistic disorder of a typical artist's workroom. In a corner, however, stood an easel with a half-finished canvas—a portrait; and several paintings adorned the walls.

By the delicate radiance of various glass and paper patterns of artistic design, I discerned some men and women who all rose to greet us as we entered. I recognized Emma at first glance. She rose and strolled leisurely toward Gina, looking directly at us with unnaturally dilated and strikingly bright pupils. She wore something more akin to a veil than a dress, beneath whose light, clinging folds of steely blue tint, the contours of her body, devoid of any other garment, were discernible. A broad Venetian girdle, intricately adorned with gold, dangled from her wide hips.

I've seen many beautiful women in my life, but upon seeing her, I was overwhelmed with admiration. The desire to laugh aloud, kneel down, and thank her for being so marvelously fair surged within me. Everything that had previously captivated me now seemed faded and lacking in color. I could never have believed that a being so majestic, reminiscent of classical antiquity, and regally more than beautiful, could exist in the real world. All that was purely natural about her was that she lived; the rest seemed like a masterpiece of painting, sculpture, and poetry combined. She was indeed more beautiful than anything in nature—be it in the azure heavens, meadows, or forests—lovelier than a midsummer night!

She greeted Gina with a kiss as she approached to welcome her. To me, she offered her hand with a courteous but chilly demeanor. Her eyes, locking onto mine, conveyed a sense of distrust and scrutiny, despite her efforts to appear icily serene.

The other woman in attendance undoubtedly belonged to "good society": a pleasant, attractive, dreamy blonde. Radłowski, in introducing us, skillfully avoided mentioning her name. She was from high society, and so had to remain incognito at this gathering. All the men were already familiar to me by name: two painters, a few literary men, and a poet. Like Emma, they too had unnaturally dilated pupils; Radłowski, Gina, and the unnamed lady shared this peculiar trait.

Upon getting acquainted with these individuals, I noted, not without pleasant surprise, that all the collars were immaculate, none turned down; not one tie was eccentric, and not a head of hair was superabundant. On the contrary, their attire was tasteful, their behavior unassuming, and their demeanor quietly refined. In the midst of this company, Emma was a much greater anachronism—twice as striking, twice as fantastical.

They spoke in hushed tones; no one contradicted, no one became excited. There was no general conversation, only a few utterances here and there. They talked neither of literature nor painting; life and the present day were their sole subjects. Their discourse revolved around frivolous or ordinary matters, articulated with elaborate elegance. Their manner of taking things, their tone and temperament, immediately revealed the kind of people they were. They belonged to those who had moved beyond the past—the stress and tumult of Decadentism—and had arrived at some form of fragmentary synthesis that they established as their standard. Their mental equilibrium bestowed upon them an extraordinary excellence of form, a philosophical calm in their worldview, and an ecstatic reverence for life, which, from their perspective, almost equated to the Beautiful. They were characterized by great enlightenment, mental distinction, contempt for all unsightly mediocrity, a picturesque way of life, and an inexpressibly artistic and restful moderation—reminiscent of the Greek soul.

One of the painters exclaimed, "I'd like to remind Emma of the promise she made us last night, which was so gratifying to us all."

"Ah, yes, we are all expectant."

"Emma is something of a littérateur and writes poetry," explained a slender fair-haired young man beside me.

An exception to the universal custom occurred; he made no bashful excuses.

"As you wish," she said.

With exquisite grace in every movement, she rose from the sofa and traversed the studio slowly, allowing us to feast our enchanted eyes on the spectacle of her fairy-like beauty.

Enamored, not unlike Narcissus, of her own splendid form, radiant with her lofty, queen-like head, perfectly molded shoulders, and cream-hued limbs just visible beneath the clinging fabric she wore, she came to a standstill opposite me. With a motion as harmoniously entrancing as a strain of music, she adjusted the golden fillet on her superbly chiseled Pagan brow and began her recitation.

In love, the Ice-Queen reigns, enchanted and spell-bound,
Strings of cold pearls cascade from her icy throne.
In her frozen cisterns, weirdly blossoming flowers,
And in chilly grottoes, flames of gold unfold.

Tonight, I deciphered the stars' Runic riddle:
There, on Life's verdant banks—alas!
Someone has torn apart the sepulchral shroud,
Under which Sleep now lies in eternal rest.

Why should I impatiently await the morning,
When it's written that I shall expire at dawn?
Yet, for my distraught heart still loves Life ardently,
Today, I summon my true love to me!

Come to me, dear one! Greet me, but in silence,
Do not awaken the sleeping ghosts of sad Memory.
Gently lower the ice-cold curtains,
Quietly draw aside the silken veils.

Enter my tent, though darkness surrounds us,
Fear not; soft stars twinkle above;
(Oh, how my wings of silver long to join them!):
Shield your eyes, love, from the fearsome black night!

Will you share clusters—grapes with warm blood swelling?
Lay your golden head between my breasts!
Let your arms, mighty with youth's keen transport,
Enfold me in embraces like a serpent's coil.

Here is no boundless sky vault;
No stars gleam against the blue expanse.
My silken tresses form a tent, stars shining bright:
Only my eyes are true constellations.

Take my blood, take all that I am,
Give me my memories, my bygone sleep!
I had a dream that froze my fountains of joy—
A dream with dim ghosts and muffled sobs!

Dreams are but dreams! Do you see the sun's red circle?
Huge, tinged with gore on the early dawn?
Your lips—oh, how I love them, crimson roses,
Royally purple, and solely mine!

My wings are broken; at your feet, I lay them
(Once soaring high in the airy void, now broken):
Oh, how I love You! You are a golden garland,
Glinting resplendent in my silky hair!

The recitation concluded, she gave us a casual salute, and a gold bracelet gleamed above the elbow of her bare arm. Then she reclined on the nearest sofa, adorned with a richly patterned throw. No gratitude was expected or offered. There she lay, hands clasped beneath her head, black diamonds of her eyes fixed steadfastly upon the ceiling.

"Oh, the heavenly bliss I am beginning to feel now!" a sudden thought flashed across my mind.

Yes, the narcotic was already taking effect. All that was negative, painful, or imperfect within me had vanished. I was filled with light—a chilly splendor, supremely disdainful of all things, supremely blissful.

The chill had enveloped me. The wide-open, tranquil eyes of all those men, gazing as in a hypnotic trance upon the miracle of female beauty before them, emitted an uncanny greenish light, like certain gases in slow combustion. We were in an atmosphere of superhuman delight; a delight not of this world, the eternally fascinating delight of non-Existence.

There was a listening to the silence, an attention riveted and petrified. The slightest murmur of life caused discomfort. No one was permitted into the studio; Radłowski and Gina poured black coffee and served it to each of us. Soft and low, words as delicate as silken tissue fell slowly from our lips, containing thoughts of subtle essence, hidden in mystery.

The unknown blonde said to Emma:

"In moments like these, I never think of my lover. I wish to feel no love for him, so I may dream of Love itself. I see a land not found on earth: where a Not-sun shines, and where Not-flowers exude fragrance! A vision! I behold a lover not of this world, and him alone I love. In a vision. In my slumbers!"

"There is nothing in the world," said Emma, "so beautiful as that which is not in it. Oh, how sweet is the longing for love that cannot be found!"

We all experienced an extraordinary and ecstatic glow, where nothing seemed too naïve or too exalted.

I felt a warm inclination toward these people, a deep gratitude because they were all in such harmony with one another. It was almost pure ideal friendship, founded on a shared appreciation and disdain, uniting those of the same caste: a cool and egotistical friendship that one demigod might feel for another.

The slender young man leaned toward me:

"Please, tell me something about love."

"Love? I know only one kind."

"And what is that?"

"The fanatical, the Pagan love of Self."

I clasped my hands and rested my head upon them. Gazing into that infinite distance where all is rigid, where no motion is possible, and partly unaware of what I was saying, I spoke thus:

"Oh! How I love myself in all my manifestations! In all my loves and abhorrences; in all my dreamings and scornings; in all those most mournful victories of my own unconquerable strength! Ah! How willingly would I die this very night, this wonderful night of the blossoming and perishing of my desires!"

From one instant to the next, my feelings grew stranger and stranger. Something akin to dread was now taking hold of me. Somewhere—far, far away, as if down at the very bottom of the gulf of Life—I heard a carriage clatter past, and a shudder of unutterable dismay shook me. Unwittingly, I drew closer to my next neighbor. Presently, I felt the soothing, almost spiritual caress of someone's cool white hand passing over my forehead. As it gently stroked me, my alarms were dispelled, and again, I was steeped in that phosphorescent celestial luminosity, as if of gases in slow combustion.

And now it returned, that vision, that majestic long-forgotten vision. Once more, I saw around me the endless stretches of the icy plains. The sun was not visible in the jet-black sky, and above the horizon rose the cold greenish glimmer of the Northern Lights. And behold, those cold dead dreams of mine had come to life again!

There is no longer any Ego of mine. I am beyond existence and beyond nothingness—in that world wherein dies the immemorial conflict between dream and vigil, where Evil, robed in her queenly purple, is no longer shadowed by Vengeance, attired in pallid green; where stony Hatred no longer hugs in her fierce embrace the weeping god of love; where the marble statue of Pride no more does homage to the grim specter, Fear; wherein there are no more wretched victories, nor the portentous delights of worshipping Self and the Power of Self!

And I am in such ecstasy—ecstasy so ethereal, so divine!

That?—Oh, *that*? It has faded away. Only occasionally.

Yes, every now and then, I discard all remnants of kisses from the past—set aside my wreath of plush purple flowers—and go, strolling calmly and unhurriedly, under the cold light of the moon, to kneel at the grave where my dreams lie buried, pressing my forehead against the base of the tombstone that shelters them, and reflect.

Once, I hung a wreath of snow-white lilies there; now, I refrain from doing so. I no longer bring any flowers to that tomb.

Nor do I attempt to move the gray stone from the sepulcher—that stone, with its ancient black fern-patterned engraving.

Then I return home and once again dress myself in my plush purple flowers.

Fragrance, beyond description, a wild and fatal scent of withered roses! Sweet, most sweet, and passionate lips—lips now lost forever! Ah, that heavenly being, with arms like pale dead gold!

All of this—I can no longer determine whether it was a dream or not.

Ah! but what is this? Have the cool white lilies blossomed once again in my abandoned garden?

A dream!—A dream!

The hand, with its pure white hue,
Longs eagerly to sway,
Yet the silent bell it cradles,
Shall never chime or play.

But why then am I so immensely, so divinely happy?

Those eyes, dim, sweet, and sad, of him who once was mine! I can no longer say whether it was all a dream, or not. My plains of ice once more, my plains of ice! No… before these… still farther back! still farther! Another, and a far different, sweet smell: a fresh delicious perfume—of meadows in flower, of willow tassels, of the lilacs in blossom.—Yellow marigolds! (O heavens, those strange far-off memories!) O sunshine, O green fields, O adorable bygone days! O my childhood!

Tears flow in torrents—tears for the sunshine, for life, for happiness. Do not wipe my eyes, for they are dropping pearls! Why brush those pearls away?

That hand, pristine in its white hue,
Oh, may it never swing to pursue,
The bell that cannot chime and sing,
A deep rift holds a hushed offering.

I woke up long after daybreak. Gina was leaning over me.

"Let's get out of here," she said. "You're a bit shaken. It's normal the first time. You need to get used to it."

A tall woman, draped in a long mantle of white fur from head to foot, awaited us. Her complexion had a muddy yellowish hue, and her eyes seemed dull and sodden. It took more than one glance for me to recognize her.

A grey-haired gentleman, whom I couldn't recall ever seeing before, accompanied us to the carriage.

I shielded my eyes with my hands, reluctant to face the world any longer.

And thus, my hymn of love concludes. I had informed Śmiłowicz that I intended to visit the Professor, and I did so today.

Returning to those solemn-looking rooms, lined with books up to the ceiling, and encountering the same beautiful old man, now a bit older, stirred a peculiar feeling within me.

He greeted me with joy. "My prodigal daughter," he said, "is even dearer to me now than before!"

Maintaining complete silence about the rupture wouldn't have sufficed for his kindness.

"Do not think I am entirely disinterested in wanting you back," he continued. "I have something specific in mind."

"What is it, Professor?"

"I've received permission from the Russian Government to publish a scientific journal, and I've been confirmed as the editor. As my secretary, you would be useful, and I invite you to take the position."

"I would be pleased, but my current occupation is a hindrance."

"Your office? You will give it up. It's not a suitable position for you. This is the ideal way to fully utilize your abilities. Initially, you'll handle the 'Intelligence' columns, provide summaries, and write translations. You'll also need to read a lot. I have numerous new and highly interesting works that I must share with you. Well, what do you say?"

I agreed.

During our conversation, I felt the same way I did when visiting Madame Śmiłowicz. I was no longer "up-to-date" since I had given up reading long ago. Obojański extensively discussed various changes in his field of science over the last few years.

Those lost years had cost me dearly. Abandoning the "Plains of ice" had not enriched my understanding of life; I was unable to formulate any synthesized views about it. The more we learn, the less comprehensible life becomes in any systematized generalization. Everything in life contradicts everything else, whereas science maintains more consistency.

"But," Obojański inquired, "what brought about your return?"

"Śmiłowicz."

"I don't mean that. There must be something deeper, some change in your mind and views, right?"

He probably expected to hear romantic phrases about the emptiness of the years and the failure of life to bring me happiness.

Instead, I surprised him with this response:

"Well, overall, it's because I choose to come back to you, whom I've departed from, rather than returning to the Church!"

Obojański looked at me in bewilderment.

THE END

Notes

---

[1] Henri Frédéric Amiel (1821-1881) was a Swiss moral philosopher, poet, and critic.

[2] Hulda Garborg (1862-1934) was a Norwegian writer, folk dancer, and women's rights activist.

[3] Ellen Karolina Sofia Key (1849-1926) was a Swedish difference feminist and suffragist.

[4] "without fear or reproach"

[5] A Polish folk and ballroom dance with origins in the region of Mazovia.

[6] A Russian measure of length, about 0.66 of a mile.

[7] "Azoic," is the state of having no trace of life or organic remains. It is an out of use term for "Archean," which is the eon that constitutes the earlier (or middle) part of the Precambrian eon.

[8] Marcus Aurelius Antoninus (204 -222), or "Elagabalus," was Roman emperor from 218 to 222, while still a teenager. His short reign was notorious for sex scandals and religious controversy.

[9] "the veiled lady"

[10] "devil take it!"

[11] Enrico Ferri (1856-1929) was an Italian criminologist and socialist. Unlike others who researched the purported physiological factors that motivated criminals, Ferri investigated social and economic aspects.

[12] "a healthy mind in a healthy body."

[13] "sadness of living"

[14] Hetaerism was a theoretical early state of human society postulated by nineteenth-century anthropologists which was characterized by the absence of the institution of marriage, and where women were the common property of their tribe, and children never knew their fathers.

[15] Cesare Lombroso (1835-1909) was an Italian eugenicist, criminologist, phrenologist, physician, and founder of the Italian school of criminology. He was the teacher of Enrico Ferri.

[16] "Whom do you love more, Jerzy: daddy or mommy?"

[17] "Because mommy never laughs."

[18] "Because youth is what it's all about."

[19] French, literally "half-world." In nineteenth-century France, the class of women considered to be of doubtful morality and social standing.

[20] "after the flood"

[21] Jacobus de Voragine (1230-1298) was an Italian chronicler and archbishop of Genoa. He was compiler of the *Golden Legend*, a collection of the legendary

lives of saints of the medieval church. It was one of the most popular religious works of the Middle Ages.

22 "in the sated beast an angel awakens"

23 A bacchic cry.

24 Arthur Schopenhauer (1788-1860) was a German philosopher. He developed an atheistic metaphysical and ethical system that rejected the contemporaneous ideas of German idealism.

25 Anna Costenoble (1866-1930) was a German artist of the Young Germany movement.

26 Young, wealthy, fashionable people.

27 "satiated"

28 "the very best"

29 Śmiłowicz was most likely arrested and sent to a Tsarist prison camp in Siberia for having written a manifesto.

30 tuberculosis

31 Jędruś is the diminutive for Andrzej.

32 "Behold the woman." A play on Pontius Pilate's "Ecce homo."

33 According to Diogenes Laërtius, when Plato was applauded for defining a human as a "featherless biped," Diogenes the Cynic plucked a chicken and brought it to Plato's Academy, saying, "Behold! I've brought you a human," and so the Academy added "with broad flat nails" to the definition.

Printed in Dunstable, United Kingdom

63539710R00109